P9-DCD-300

DAMSEL

Also by Elana K. Arnold

Infandous

What Girls Are Made Of

DAMSEL

ELANA K. ARNOLD

BALZER + BRAY

An Imprint of HarperCollins*Publishers*

Balzer + Bray is an imprint of HarperCollins Publishers.

Damsel

www.epicreads.com

Library of Congress Cataloging-in-Publication Data

Names: Arnold, Elana K., Author.

Title: Damsel / Elana K. Arnold.

Description: First edition. | New York, NY : Balzer + Bray, An Imprint of HarperCollins Publishers, [2018] | Summary: Waking up in the arms of Prince Emory, Ama has no memory of him rescuing her from a dragon's lair, but she soon discovers there is more to the legend of dragons and damsels than anyone knows and she is still in great danger.

Identifiers: LCCN 2017057175 | ISBN 9780062742322 (hardback)

Subjects: | CYAC: Fantasy. | Dragons—Fiction.

Classification: LCC PZ7.A73517 Dam 2018 | DDC [Fic]—dc23 LC record available at https://lccn.loc.gov/2017057175

Typography by Michelle Taormina

18 19 20 21 22 PC/LSCH 10 9 8 7 6 5 4 3 2 1

First Edition

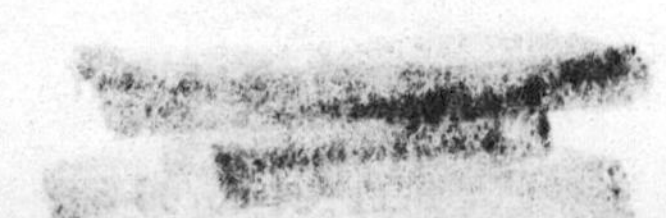

For my brother Zak, who loves dragons

ONE

The Dragon's Blame

The castle seemed to grow from the cliffs that cupped the shoreline. Its jagged-peaked turrets pierced the rain-heavy clouds above; its windows were gaping mouths and gored-out eyes. Between the slate-gray cliffs and the smoke-gray sky and the churning gray sea and the ghost-gray mist, it was a gray place, indeed. It was so thoroughly gray that a traveler who lost his way could be blinded by it—by the overwhelming grayness that permeated everything, erasing vision entirely.

Stay too long in this gray world, the legend went, and risk your eyes turning gray too. Risk your skin growing ashen. Risk your hair dulling to iron.

Yes, it was a gray world.

Sitting upon the broad back of his night-black steed, Prince Emory of Harding scanned the vast gray scene around him. There was the beach, quiet waves lapping upon the shoreline like a kitten at its dish of cream, the tameness and gentle repetition belying the fierceness Emory knew the great sea had hidden within it. There beneath his horse's hooves was a short, pebbled beach, peppered with stones of all shades of gray, from nearly black to nearly white. Emory and his steed, whom he called Reynard, had emerged onto this beach from a dense forest through which there was no trail. Emory had been obliged to lead his horse much of the way, slashing a path for them with his sword.

As Emory had grown closer to the edge of the forest, the trees he encountered grew harder and harder until, finally, he found that they were no longer made of wood at all, but rather petrified to stone. These trees even Emory's loyal, lethal sword had been powerless against, a fact that ignited a flame of anger in his chest. When he struck it, a tree should fall. That is what trees do. That is what they had always done, trees. It was their duty.

But these last trees would not fall, and when Emory struck them with his sword an awful clang rang out, and the impact of the blow vibrated up through Emory's sword arm and rattled all of his bones.

Not even a dent. Unacceptable.

Yet he had been forced to accept it, had been forced to unsaddle Reynard so the horse was narrow enough to pick a path through the trees that refused to get out of their way.

No matter, Emory had told himself as he flung the saddle back onto Reynard; as he fastened the girth, horse grunting; as he hefted himself into the saddle once again. He walked the horse along the beach, surveying, and Reynard picked a path through the pebbles. Emory would punish the forest on the dragon's flesh.

For he knew it was the dragon's blame that the trees had turned to gray stone, just as it was the dragon's blame that this part of the world was misted dark with unspilled rain, and the dragon's blame that the sea was slate gray instead of blue-green, and the dragon's blame that the unblinking eye of the sun was dulled by a cataract of gray.

When the dragon was slain (if he managed to slay it), this part of the world would brighten again, and Emory would be the light-bringer as well as king.

He hated the dragon. It was that simple, and his hate was pure like cleansing fire. He breathed in and out his hatred as he sat upon his steed, as his eyes scanned the cliffs in front of him, searching for a way to climb them, though he knew already that there would be no easy path.

Who had built this castle into these cliffs? It was a mystery without an answer. Had they built it or had it been born? Some wizened elders claimed that the castle emerged from the craggy cliffs over millennia, growing a fraction of an inch a year, surfacing so slowly that its progress was imperceptible.

Others countered that the castle had not emerged at all, but simply had always been, like the sea, like the cliffs themselves, and to attempt to trace their origin was a fool's mission.

No one knew how the castle had come to be, and Emory did not care. He did not care why a sun hung in the sky; it did, and that was enough for him. As long as it warmed his back each day and disappeared each night, Emory had no desire to waste his time examining the whys and wherefores behind its existence, and that was how he felt about the castle and the cliffs, the sea and the sky.

The world was made. That was all.

This resolved and set aside left Emory with just the question of how best to conquer it.

"I'll have to scale it, Reynard," Emory said.

The horse grunted, warm clouds puffing out from his enormous nostrils.

"You'll have to wait behind," Emory told him, to which Reynard said nothing.

That settled, Emory swung himself out of the saddle once again, landing on the shifting pebbles of the beach. They crunched together under his feet, like bones grinding.

Reynard would not need to be tied. He was a good horse, and he wouldn't go far. And if Emory did tie him, and then were to die—either falling from the cliff or in the jaws of the dragon he expected to encounter up above—Reynard would die, as well.

Everything and everyone dies, of course, but dying while tied by the reins to an outcropping of rocks at the base of a cliff seemed like an undignified way to go, and Reynard was not an undignified animal, and Emory was not, he thought, a cruel master.

Once again, Emory unhooked the long leather strap of the girth, pulling it from the brass ring at Reynard's side, unwinding it as the horse relaxed his gut. He heaved the saddle down from Reynard's proud high back, revealing a square patch of sweat-wet fur, which Emory rubbed dry with the saddle blanket. Then he grabbed the crownpiece of the bridle from behind Reynard's ears and pulled it forward, the bit clanking against the horse's teeth. Freed, Reynard stretched his neck long and wandered off, snuffling along the pebbled beach in search of the few gray tufts of sea grass.

Emory considered himself to be horselike in all the best ways. One thing he could do was place blinders on his own vision, focusing on the singular task in front of him, and this he did now, preparing himself for the climb.

The saddle and its bags were slung across a boulder, and Emory rifled through them with practiced purpose, gathering what he would need: rope; a pickax; a leather pouch of fine-powdered chalk; leather gloves; a bladder of fresh water. His sword, which was never far from his body. In his pocket was his lucky talisman, a rabbit's foot he'd cut himself from his first kill when he was seven years old.

Then he walked to the base of the cliffs, an almost-vertical wall of slate, and placed his hands on its cold, hard surface. He looked up, craning his neck farther and farther back, and for a flash it seemed that the old legend had come true, as his field of vision filled so completely with gray. So much gray, so all-encompassing, that Emory was blinded by it, and he felt his bowels loosen with fear, and for a second he was a babe again, powerless and falling, with no knowledge of what was up and what was down, drowning in the gray that whirled around him, tumbling and helpless.

But then he caught sight of his own hand against the endless gray wall, and he remembered himself. He was not powerless. He was no babe. He was Emory of Harding, and he had a dragon to slay.

Emory's Hands

The slate was tricky. It was cold, as hard and slick as ice. There were holds, but Emory found that he could not trust his vision to find them. The trick of grayness all around made this into a shadowless world, and the wall looked flat, without dimension. But if he slid his fingers along its surface, he could feel ridges, wrinkles, recesses. That was where he would grab hold, and he would make a ladder of them, an invisible chain of handholds and footholds.

And so, Emory began to climb. He had strapped his sword to his back to free his hips and legs and belted the pouch of chalk at his waist. He had tucked his black pants into his black boots and his black shirt into his pants. He had used a strip of leather to gather his hair back into a rough knot, keeping it from his eyes. He had rolled his sleeves back, in spite of the cold, knowing that he would warm as he climbed.

Hand over hand, hold after hold, Emory ascended. Always he had been a skilled climber—as well as a skilled fighter, a skilled rider, a skilled swimmer—anything he needed his body to do, it did, and well. Part of the trick was to take his mind off the task. In this, as in many things, his body knew better than his head what must happen next, and his mind's job was to keep still and let the muscles get on with it.

As if watching a stranger, Emory saw his fingers creep along the wall, touch and reject a possible hold, find a second hold, accept it, and latch on, clawlike. His feet shimmied up several inches, his biceps curled, and he was higher, fifteen feet off the ground at least, and hundreds more to go.

To keep his mind entertained while his body was working, Prince Emory of Harding allowed himself to imagine what they might be saying about him back at home.

His mother, as ever, came first into his head. He saw her sitting where she liked it best, all the year round, regardless of the temperature outside—next to the fireplace in her chambers, pressed up closer to the flames than anyone else could stand, surrounded by cushions and cats, never dogs.

"Now, Emory," she was wont to say, patting the cushions beside her, "tell me what you've conquered today."

And as a young boy, Emory would obligingly scramble up beside her, even when the heat from fire made him sweat, and report exactly what he had mastered:

The puppy he had trained to follow him through the palace grounds, simply by keeping a fatty piece of breakfast meat in his pocket.

The teacher he had talked into freeing him from lessons a quarter hour early.

The horse he had broken to saddle.

The cook he had cajoled into baking an extra cake, just for him.

Later, when he was too big to cuddle, Emory would stand across from Mother and report, just as proudly:

The buck he'd felled in Moss Forest.

The soldiers he'd rallied to fight.

The rider he'd beaten at joust.

The scholar he'd bested at chess.

Other conquests, those of the soft-skin variety, Emory did not tell Mother about, though he suspected that she both knew and approved of them:

Pink-cheeked Elaine, the cowherd's daughter.

Raven-dark Lila, who kept shop for her mother, the apothecary.

Flour-dusted kitchen apprentice Fabiana, on the heavy canvas sacks of flour in the cool dark pantry, while old Cooky pretended she didn't know what was going on.

And Mother always listened, and nodded, and approved of the things Emory said and the things he did not say in equal measure. The fire blazed, the cats purred, and Mother listened.

Emory's muscles warmed and loosened as he climbed. When

his fingers began to slip with sweat on the slate, he dipped them into the bag of chalk, its fine powdery residue recalling the flour that had puffed up, from the sacks on which they lay, from Fabiana herself, as they rutted in the pantry back at home.

But this was not a safe direction to allow his thoughts to wander. Not now, not here on this cliff, a hundred feet above the ground. From here, a fall would be death.

So Emory took Fabiana and placed her to the side, out of the way, where she belonged. He watched his left hand reach, fingertips stretched, feeling for a hold that must be there, it must, and he felt the strong muscles of his thighs and calves tremble as he pushed up onto the tips of his boots, as his right hand held tight into the good hold it had, and the fingers of his left hand were still searching when the slate beneath his right hand began to crumble.

At first the crumbling could be mistaken for just the sensation of the chalk powder rubbing against the wall, so fine was the beginning of the end. And brains don't want to believe they are imperiled. A brain will lie to the body, even when the body is the brain's only hope.

Emory had seen this, many times: the blind stare of disbelief from a buck, freezing it in place as he aimed and shot his arrow; the blank-faced shock of impending loss on the face of a fighter who, until that very moment, had been undefeated.

So he did not trust his brain's initial reasoning—*it's just chalk powder,* his brain told him. *It's fine.*

It *wasn't* fine, not fine at all, and Emory shifted his weight even farther to the left, the fingers of that hand straining and praying for purchase, as the slate beneath the right hand crumbled in earnest, the handhold disintegrating like burned bone.

For a fraction of a second, Emory held nothing—not with his left hand, nor with his right. No stone in his hands, no thoughts in his head, no hope in his heart, which did not dare to even beat in that moment, no breath in his lungs, no sight in his eyes. Suspended, still, empty.

And then he began to fall.

The Dragon's Lair

As cold as it was below, so it was warm above. As gray as it was below, so it was golden above.

On the outside, the castle was cold and gray, it was true, but inside was a different story altogether. A thousand feet above the cliff face from which Emory of Harding was falling, curled like a kitten, rested the dragon.

If you were to visit the dragon in its chambers, the first thing you would notice, of course, was the dragon itself—the enormity of it, the vastness of its spear-shaped head, the rows of opalescent scales, each the size of a tea saucer.

But what would you notice next? Well, if you were of a mercenary nature, perhaps it would be the jewels.

Great piles of jewels filled each corner, heaps of jewels spilled through each doorway, hundreds of jewels lined the walls, a rainbow of opulence—rubies rich as blood, tourmalines as bright and round as oranges, citrines yellower than the sun, emeralds as green as the greed of goblins, sapphires as blue as the brightest sea, amethysts as purple as the velvet cloak of a king.

And diamonds. Everywhere, diamonds. A veritable hoard of them.

If, on the other hand, you had emerged half frozen from the cliffs below, perhaps the jewels would not be what drew your attention. Perhaps it would be the heat.

Twin billows of steam emerged from the sleeping dragon's nostrils, thick plumes of dragon vapor. The dragon's lair was oppressive in its heat, sultry and overwhelming and boilingly hot. The air was almost hot enough and wet enough to poach an egg, if you had an egg. Almost hot enough to knock you flat.

But if you were a visitor with a Narcissus-like vanity, perhaps the heat and the jewels and maybe even the dragon itself would not be what caught your eye, first of all. For the entirety of the castle, floor to ceiling, each and every surface, was lined in mirrors—mirrors that threw golden reflections tinted with rose, mirrors that reflected mirrors and mirrors beyond that, and each of them, whichever way you turned, reflecting your reflection, again and again, forever.

And woven through it all—the jewels and the heat and the rose-gold mirrors—was a scent. A balm, a spice, an infusion. It rose on the plumes of steam; it drifted through the open windows and diffused into the grayness outside.

And it was this scent that Emory of Harding inhaled as his handhold turned to dust and as he began to fall.

He didn't have time to think about the scent in words. If he kept falling, in a few seconds he would be dead. But somewhere in his brain the scent took hold. It matched like a key in a lock and opened up a memory.

He was a child. No—an infant baby newly born. No—before that, even. He was womb-bound, eyes unopened, breathing and swimming in the hot stew of his mother's juice. He could taste it and smell it, the same sweet-spice tang, then and again now, here, from above.

His left hand grabbed the pickax from his waist and struck it blindly at the slate-gray wall. And though it shouldn't have, though the chances were nearly naught, the pick found purchase, a slit in the rock just the width of the pickax's blade.

Emory's fingers slid down the worn wood handle, and he was almost lost again, but he clenched his fist even tighter and then he stopped, hanging and swinging by one arm, the joint of his shoulder nearly torn asunder.

He breathed again, but the scent, and the memory, were gone. He brought his right hand up to meet his left, found holds for one foot and then the other, closed his eyes and bent his head for just a moment in thanks and prayer—to the gods, but also to his own strength and quickness. And then he grasped the wall again with his right hand, pulled the pickax free with his left, and resumed his climb.

At the top of the cliff in the womb-warm room, surrounded by mirrors and jewels and clouds of its own exhaled heat, the dragon opened one amber eye.

Pawlin's Hawk

His strong right hand was the first part of Emory to make it, hours later, to the top of the cliff. Trembling, his right arm bent, hoisting the rest of Emory—his sweat-darkened head, strands of hair escaping from the leather tie, his straining, reddened face, his wide shoulders, his chest, his narrow waist, the crux of him, and then his legs and feet.

It was like being born new, emerging from over the edge of the cliff, and, like a newborn, Emory wanted to rest and wail and suck up air. He lay on the gray slate ground and felt every muscle burning, every joint on fire, his lungs working in shallow pants, greedy for air but too weak to take in all they needed.

He wanted to retch. He wanted to faint. But instead, he stood. He stood as tall and as wide as he could, and he turned his face in the direction of the castle, and he smiled, flashing his teeth.

For like all good hunters, Emory knew when he was being hunted. And he felt the dragon's amber eye upon him as surely as the sun. Then, knowing the dragon was watching, he unbuttoned the front of his trousers, freed his yard, and pissed a steaming stream right there, at the top of the cliff, marking it as his own.

That accomplished, retucked and rebuttoned, Emory approached the castle.

At home, all of Harding would be resting after their noontime meal. The ladies would be in their chambers, loosening their stays to aid digestion, the older women gathering in circles around their handiwork, the girls piling together on the tall curtained beds to laugh and gossip.

The men and boys would be out of doors, if the day was fine, sporting with the horses or the hounds or perhaps playing at swords with the younger boys.

Of course, the servants would be neither resting nor playing, but rather working, as was their duty—clearing away the noon meal, beginning the preparations for supper, carrying water from the well, beating rugs free of dust, shoveling manure from the pigs' sty, and all the other labors that Emory was only aware of when someone had failed to do them.

If he were home right now, Emory would perhaps be walking the fence line with Pawlin, the falconer, who would himself be accompanied by Isolda, his hawk, who would perch, as she always did, on

Pawlin's leather gauntlet, her leather jesses streaming like ribbons from her legs.

Isolda would listen as Pawlin bragged about everything: the hunt of the day before, the conquest of the night before, the hardiness of Pawlin's erection—"like the blacksmith's hammer, it was"—and Emory would listen too, and laugh, for Pawlin was as clever as he was loyal, and an afternoon spent in his company was sure to be entertaining.

But Emory was not home. He was not flanked by friendship and laughter. There was no ease here, on the cliffs before this great gray castle. There was no good meal in his belly, or wine in his cup. There was no cup.

Emory took his water bladder from his side and sucked like a babe at the teat until it was empty. If he were to die in that castle, there would be no need for more water. For in spite of his bravado, his great hot jet of urine, and the strong square of his shoulders, Emory was afraid.

"And why wouldn't you be?" Emory heard Pawlin's voice echo in his head. "You'd be a damned idiot not to be scared. For God's balls, there's a *dragon* up there!"

Imagining Pawlin beside him helped Emory relax a bit. For Pawlin would have found a way to make even a situation as grim as the one into which Emory had placed himself seem a lark.

Yes, Pawlin was there, just to his right. And Isolda as well, with her ever-disdainful expression, eager to be loosed from Pawlin's arm and ready to gore out an amber eye with her ferocious beak, if need be.

He was not alone.

I am not alone, Emory told himself. He had arrived, alone, at the great door of the dragon's castle. At its base, looking up, Emory felt almost as overwhelmed as he had at the base of the cliff. Such a door—broad as two men laid head to toe, and tall as ten. Gray, but not cold—even before he touched it, Emory felt the heat that radiated off the door, generated, no doubt, by the dragon within.

He laid his hand flat against the door and immediately withdrew it. Hot, hot, too hot. He pulled his gloves from the waistband of his pants and drew them on. Fine black leather gloves, sewn just for him by his mother. She had given the gloves to him from the chair by her fire when he had gone to kiss her good-bye.

"My fine young man," she had said, "let us speak honestly with one another. You are no longer a boy, but you are just barely a man. You are a skilled fighter, that is the truth, but dragons are bigger and tougher than even the best of men."

It had hurt, to hear his mother speak so, but it had felt good, too, like when a boil is lanced—pain, mixed with relief.

"I know my chances," Emory had said. "But what is my choice?"

For Emory's father was dead, two fortnights now, from a spreading madness some said had started with his early affection for whores, before he had married Emory's mother, and which had gone dormant for many years, reemerging just last winter when his muscles began to seize, his face began to sag, his eyes began to cloud, and he began to shout loudly, whether anyone listened or not, that the dragon was coming, that it would feast on Emory's heart, that the dragon was coming, was coming, was coming, until, at last, his screaming stopped and he was dead.

The king should have lived another ten years—maybe another twenty. And with that time, Emory would have trained. He would have prepared, the best he could. With Pawlin at his side, and all the aid and assistance of Harding's best fighters, Emory would have grown stronger, and faster, and surer of foot, and deadlier.

The truth was that the king's early death had stolen years of preparation from Emory.

It mattered not to the people of Harding that Emory must face a dragon before he had even reached his twentieth year, though his forbearers, as far back as history remembered, had made it to nearly thirty before each faced his dragon. For Emory to take his father's place as king, he must do as his father had done, and his father before him. He must conquer a dragon and rescue a damsel, and take that maiden as his bride. And he must do so without having been given any instruction in the ways of dragons, and he must do it single-handedly, without aid from any quarter. For so it had been throughout his people's memory, that *a dragon and a damsel made a king*.

"Your chances may be slim," the queen mother said, who had herself once been a rescued maiden, "but your choices, as you say, are slimmer. So, take these gloves." And she handed them into Emory's grasp, and he took them. They were heavier than they looked to be, and the leather, though soft, was thick. "These will protect your hands against the dragon's heat," she said. "They are half of what I have to offer, and they are not enough," she went on. "So listen to what else I have to say. Your sword is one weapon. Your mind is another. But you have a third, and to conquer the dragon you shall need all three."

Emory had looked deep into his mother's dark eyes, waiting for her to tell him what his third weapon was, but something in him told him not to ask. He had nodded as if he had understood, and thanked her for the gloves, and kissed her cheek, and walked away, leaving her in her chamber by the fire, a ginger cat curled in her lap.

The gloves were on his hands. His sword was at his hip. His brain was in his head. Whether or not Emory had the other weapon, the one his mother had told him he would need . . . well, it no longer mattered, did it? For Emory watched his hand push against the door and he heard it moan open, and then he stepped inside the dragon's castle.

The Devil's Eye

Emory was a warrior first, and so the dragon was the first thing he saw. Nothing else mattered except how it would figure in battle: the debilitating heat mattered only in the challenge it would pose to Emory's stamina; the heaping jewels mattered only in how the piles of them might provide protection, how they might be useful as weapons; the mirrors he noted as a strike in the dragon's favor, for surely the dragon was used to their deception, though Emory was not.

The scent—the sweet-spice tang that he could not see but was as real as everything else in the great castle hall—the scent, he took care to not breathe in too deeply, for perhaps it was poisonous.

Sword unsheathed, held steady in front of him, Emory assessed his enemy. Why a creature this repugnant would choose to line its lair in reflective glass, Emory could not begin to guess. For though its opalescent scales were what drew a man's gaze, the skin around the dragon's eye slits and nostrils was puce, like dried blood; and the claws on the dragon's front feet, which it had crossed in front of itself like a housecat, were each a black, serrated, menacing hook that could tease the guts from a man with the gentlest stroke.

From where he stood, Emory could see but one of the dragon's eyes, and it was closed. Great bursts of steam billowed from the dragon's nostrils; the mirrored walls dripped with condensation. The beast had holes instead of ears. The tips of black teeth gleamed along the edges of its lipless reptilian mouth. A tongue flicked out—forked, black, awful—and disappeared.

And then Emory looked past the beast's head, into the mirror behind it. Slitted, unblinking, amber—the reflection of the dragon's other eye—open, watching.

Emory gasped, his breath catching like a death rattle, for in that moment he knew that he would die. He knew it, sure as he'd been about anything ever before, and he wished suddenly with a fervor that he was just a boy again.

In the dragon's amber gaze, Emory saw the sun of his seventh summer. For the hottest three days of that summer, in mid-August, some strange celestial event had cast a shadow across the middle of the sun—a long slit, it looked like, that transformed the sun Emory had always known into a cruel reptilian eye.

Devil's eye, the priests called it, kissing the sharp-tipped triangles they wore on chains about their necks, and they warned everyone to stay inside, away from its unblinking watch.

But Emory's father, the king, did not abide such hogswallop. "Come, son," he said on the hottest of the three days, the last. "We shall hunt."

And he waved away the squires and the footmen and the master of the hounds, taking only a paring knife from the kitchen, two apples, and Emory's own small bow and quiver of arrows.

Young Emory followed his father away from the castle and keep, the weight of the devil's eye heavy on his head, and he followed his father through the gate in the wall, and on, until they reached the forest, dappled and shadowed and hushed, where the eye could not see him anymore.

The king was a big man, broad and handsome, with skin tanned to leather, feet and hands callused from battle and from play. At seven, Emory already fashioned his hair after his father's, worn down in loose black curls to please the ladies when at court and tied back with a strip of leather when afield. The king's strong brow meant he never had to squint against the sun, and his full mouth was never afraid to laugh, to kiss, to eat, to cry. He was a man who held life in his jaws as a dog held a smoked lamb's leg—with devourous greed and absolute pleasure.

On this day, he would teach his son, his first and only child, how to kill. What a pleasant way to spend a summer afternoon!

Emory carried his own quiver across his shoulder, his own bow in his hand. He had unloaded his small shafts many times into targets and practice dummies, to the applause and praise of his teachers, and with his quiver over his shoulder and his father at his side—and now that he was hidden by trees from the devil's eye—he felt himself very brave indeed. He imagined that he and his father were two of a pair, both big, both strong, both rulers of their world. He followed his father and made a game of stepping just where his father had stepped before him, hopping from place to place, since the king's stride was easily three times the length of his own. It was cooler in the forest, away from the sun's reach, and Emory was happy.

Suddenly, his father stopped. Emory stopped too, just barely before crashing into the king's back. "There," said the king, and he pointed not twenty feet away, near the base of a tall fir tree, at a light-brown hare.

Emory did not hesitate. He reached over his left shoulder with his right hand, plucked an arrow from the quiver, notched it in his bow, and, with an exhale, loosed it.

The hare looked up and locked its gaze with Emory's. Its eyes, jewel black and shiny, did not blink. The hare knew it was too late to hope for mercy, and Emory knew it was too late to call back his arrow, though if he could have, he would not.

The arrow struck the hare in its neck, piercing through the front and coming out the other side. Blood stained its white scruff red, and it was dead before Emory had run to its body.

He stared down at the rabbit, at the eyes that had just been alive with shine a second before, and now were dull with death. The king's heavy, callused hand landed with a thump on Emory's shoulder. "Well done, my son," he said.

And then he handed Emory the paring knife and said, "Choose the best foot." Emory selected the right rear, because he himself favored his right hand, and because the rear foot was where a hare held its power. His father the king watched as Emory sawed through the still-warm fur, meat, tendon, and bone to retrieve his talisman. Then the king took the paring knife.

Emory watched him slit an opening in the rabbit's fur and set aside the knife. The king glided his pointer and middle fingers of both hands into the hole he'd made, and he pulled, and with a sound like cloth tearing, the rabbit's pelt pulled away, revealing the white shiny membrane underneath and, beneath that, the red muscles and white tendons and bones. The king tore the pelt all the way open, to the head and remaining hind foot, then he snapped the foot easy as could be, sawed though the neck, and pulled the pelt the rest of the way free. He flipped the rabbit belly-side up, made a shallow cut just through the thin white skin, slipped his fingers underneath to lift the skin away from the intestines, and then cut all the way up the length of the rabbit. Pulling open the skin, he carefully retrieved the heart, placing it into Emory's cupped hands.

"It's your heart, son," he said. "Do you want to eat it now, or later, after Cooky can fry it up?"

Emory stared down at the raw red thing he was holding. He

knew his father wanted him to eat it now, raw and fresh from the rabbit's chest. But the thought of swallowing such a warm slimy thing, like a large red slug, made him feel as if he might vomit. "Later, please," he said, and if the king was displeased, he did not show it.

He turned back to his work, quickly spilling the intestines into the dirt and scooping the liver, kidneys, and lungs, then the heart from Emory's hands, into a leather pouch.

What was left of Emory's kill looked like meat, now, rather than rabbit, and Emory's mouth began to water. How pleased Mother would be!

Then the king had given Emory an apple to eat on the walk home, and he let Emory lead the way.

Now, here in the dragon's lair, seeing the reflected amber eye watching him, Emory remembered. He had been afraid of the devil's eye when he had entered the forest, and though it still had hung in the sky when he emerged, with the hare's foot in his pocket and his first kill behind him, it was no longer the devil's eye that hung in the sky, not to Emory; it was only a trick of shadow and light, and nothing more.

"Dragon," he said, the talisman from a decade ago snug in his pocket, "I am here to conquer you." Perhaps he would die today. Perhaps he would live. Either way, he would not hesitate. He would not falter.

A dragon is a big and scary thing, but it is not the only big and scary thing. Emory had seen others. Perhaps this monstrosity before him was like the devil's eye from his childhood: made bigger and scarier by fear and ignorance, cut down and put into its place with perspective and knowledge.

The dragon opened its other eye and turned its giant head. And then it opened its jaws, black teeth and black forked tongue, and it roared a deafening screech that vibrated Emory's skeleton.

Or, Emory reconsidered, perhaps not.

Emory's Sword

Emory held his weapon waist-high, perpendicular to the ground, cutting his field of vision into two equal parts. He shifted his weight from right to left and back again, testing the beast's response to his movement. Its gaze, he noted, did follow him, but slowly, as if it didn't see him well, or clearly.

In his kingdom, no one would speak to Emory about dragons; all his life, he had known that one day he would face a dragon unaided and untaught. But still, he heard things from time to time: servants telling tales, stories bandied about at market. And though he had no real study of dragons on which to depend, he'd heard it said that dragons have vision only for far and not for close, and other times that the dragons' deep love of gold and jewels comes from their attraction for brightly colored things. This had all seemed like the senseless talk of those who would never themselves meet a dragon in close quarters and had nothing better to do with their idle time than chatter, but seeing this creature's unfocused gaze gave Emory hope that, perhaps, there was some truth to the old legends, after all.

Then his steel blade caught a glint of sunlight through the window, and the dragon's focus shifted in an instant, becoming razor sharp, and it drew itself up on its haunches, claws tapping the mirrored floor, and stepped toward him.

It was the brightness that drew the dragon's gaze! Emory shifted his sword so the sun no longer struck it, and he stepped back as the dragon opened its maw. He had half a second before a jet of blue flame sprayed out, and he leaped away, rolling behind a mountain of jewels just in time.

He had to dull the shine of his blade. Emory looked about, desperate, but all around him were jewels and reflections of jewels, and reflections of his own panicked visage, the color high in his cheeks.

But, there—at his reflection's waist! The bag of chalk he'd used when climbing. Emory dug a handful of powder from the bag, its dry coolness coating his fingers, such a contrast to the hall's humid heat, and he rubbed it across the blade, turning his sword from hilt to tip a dull gray-white.

The hand he'd dipped in the chalk had been transformed, as well, its bronze skin well masked, and so Emory dug into the bag again, scooping up another fistful of chalk, and he rubbed it into his cheeks, his forehead, his chin, his nose, his neck, turning himself into a ghost, a shadow warrior.

As a test, he found a gem, a ruby the size of an apple, and rolled it away from the pile as quietly as he could. The dragon's smart amber gaze was upon it at once, tracking its progress across the floor.

Then, his heart pounding in his throat, Emory extended his arm from behind the jewel heap where he crouched, waiting for the dragon's breath to scorch it.

Nothing. Emory wiggled his fingers. Again, nothing. Drawing his hand back, Emory sighed his relief.

There was naught wrong with the dragon's hearing, Emory instantly learned as the beast charged the jewel stack with a roar, sending gems flying to clatter in all directions, striking the mirrored walls in a series of bangs and crashes. Silent as a ghost, Emory slipped along the wall to the far side of the chamber, and the dragon did not follow.

The mirrors all around were not made of glass. They were instead highly polished sheets of gold that reflected almost as clearly as a looking glass, but with a strange rosy tint that he could not explain.

There were panels in the mirrors, Emory saw, panels that meant there were rooms beyond this one. Rooms in which a damsel must be hidden. Was she suffering, he wondered, his fated beauty? Was she locked and chained? Was she frightened? She was somewhere, Emory knew, and he would find her.

But first he must focus here, in this room, on this foe. He trained his mind back to his immediate surroundings.

Now that he had proved true the chatter he'd heard about a dragon's vision, Emory racked his brain for anything else he may have ever heard about the beasts.

"Not many places you can stick a dragon," Thad, the pig boy, had told his fellow slop-hands. It was early evening, just before sunset, and Emory and Maddie, the hedge warder's niece, were trying their best to stay silent in the hayloft where he had just relieved her of her virginity.

"Aw, Thad, you don't know shite about dragons," said little Merle, hefting his bucket of scraps up into the trough.

"Do too!" Thad shouted. "I know a sight more than you fools, I 'spect!"

"'Spect all you want," said Merle's older brother Darro. "You don't know shite about shite."

"I know shite about your sister's titties!" Thad yelled, and then Darro swung his slop pail at Thad's head, and Merle jumped into the fight, and then the three slop boys were in the mud alongside the pigs.

Emory and Maddie did their best to stifle each other's laughter, Emory's hand across Maddie's mouth, his face buried in Maddie's naked breasts. When the three boys finally broke apart and headed back toward their hut, Maddie said, "Everybody knows the only place to pierce a dragon is in the soft skin under its arm." As soon as the words were out, she gasped and clasped her hands over her mouth in a pretty gesture.

And then Emory had set into showing Maddie how much fun she could have, relieved as she was of the responsibility of virginity, and he had forgotten all about dragons.

But now, in the dragon's lair, emboldened by his success with the chalk, Emory eyed the dragon's form, and he wondered if Maddie had perhaps been right.

The Dragon's Armpit

Had Emory not been intent on killing, he may have been able to see what a spectacular achievement of artistic beauty the commencing battle was to take place in. But, warrior that he was, he saw the great hall only for what he needed from it: places to hide, a network of assets and liabilities.

Stacks of jewels: double asset.

Reflective surfaces: liability.

Such a perspective left no room for wonder.

Perhaps this was not the time for wonder, or perhaps it is always, always time for wonder, no time more so than when one's very life is facing the very real possibility of immediate termination.

In any case, had Emory been someone else, he would have seen that his reluctant host was an artist of incomparable talent. The dragon's was the art of arrangement: the gem towers were not random, mercenary stacks thrown together without regard for aesthetics. They were carefully constructed dances of color, shape, and light, and each of them told a story, called forth an emotion: Here, in citrines and diamonds, a monument to spring, and hope, and youth. There, in rubies of all shades and shapes, an angry roar and blood spilled in battle. Under a wide window, a twisting river in emeralds and sapphires, dotted with diamonds to make the water glint.

The great hall was a sanctuary; the gems, its altar.

To Emory, it was but a battleground. He plucked from the river a fist-sized emerald cylinder and threw it, hard, at the pyramid of rubies.

It crashed down, decimating the carefully constructed arrangement of crimson gems, and the dragon turned in that direction, a roar tearing from its throat.

Emory heard the anger in the dragon's roar, but his ears—like the dragon's eyes—did not perceive the whole truth. For he did not hear the dragon's anguish. He did not hear its grief. He did not consider why the dragon might drop its head, might close its eyes. All he saw was an enemy and an opportunity. The dragon's flank turned toward him, its attention to the ruined, Emory scanned its body, looking for a place where its scales did not protect it.

Emory thought that while Maddie had been wrong about wanting to keep her virginity, she had been quite right about the vulnerability of a dragon's armpit. For there, with its great front legs stretched forward, was a thin slit of scaleless dragon skin, dull dark red, a perfect target for his sword.

He would have one shot—that was all. If his sword missed its mark, the dragon would kill him. Now was not the time for brain; that had been earlier, when he disguised the sword's shine and the color of his own flesh. Now was the time for steel.

He raced forward, leaped, sword arm back, landed just behind the dragon's left front leg, and thrust true, his sword sinking deep inside the dragon's exposed red flesh. A truer mark had never been hit.

The dragon roared, and this time Emory heard it rightly—more anger, mixed with pain. It whipped around, and Emory, who hung tight to his sword handle, swung like a puppet from its side. Then his sword shifted in the meat of the beast, digging deeper, yes, but also listing to the side, and its hilt rubbed against the sharp armor of the dragon's scales.

A terrible screech rang out from the clash of steel against scale, but the dragon is mightier than the sword, and the scale's razor edge snapped his shaft.

He fell from the dragon's side, sword pommel still in hand, the blade still inside the creature's body.

He landed with an "oof," which he immediately regretted, as the sound of it alerted the dragon to his position. But it was currently engaged with the remainder of his sword in its side, attempting to bite it out. The steel was in a tricky spot, just out of easy reach, so

Emory had a moment to regroup. He rolled himself behind what he failed to recognize as a self-portrait of the dragon, rendered in diamonds and opals. There he lay, staring up at himself reflected down from the rose-gold ceiling.

The dragon writhed in worry, thrashing upon the floor of the chamber. Its mighty tail smashed one of the last remaining sculptures, and jewels scattered in a confusion of color and sound. As the beast snapped at the protruding bit of blade, Emory clenched his fist.

He had used his brain.

He had used his steel.

His mother the queen had said, "Your sword is one weapon. Your mind is another. But you have a third, and to conquer the dragon you shall need all three."

And suddenly, certainly, Emory knew what his third weapon was and what he must do.

TWO

The Prince's Belt

When the damsel woke, it was to a gentle rocking. The awareness of her naked limbs pressed one against another. An arm around her. A hard surface beneath her.

She did not open her eyes. She was not certain she wanted to see where she was. Perhaps she could stay just like this forever, curled into an uncomfortable ball, moving, yes, but without knowledge of where or why.

Because it might not be better to know these things, a voice in her head warned, one she did not yet recognize as her own. Ignorance, perhaps, would be the safer path.

But still, she peeked open her eyes—just for a second, for the light was too much to bear. Shocked by the brightness, she squeezed her eyes tight and pulled up her arm to shade them. That was when she first knew that she was not alone—by the arm and hand that relaxed to allow her to adjust her position, to shade her own eyes.

"You wake!" said a voice. Deep, rich, pleased. "Thank gods, you wake."

Then he jerked his other hand, said, "Reynard, whoa," and the rocking motion stopped.

A horse, then, and a rider.

She did not know where these words—horse, rider—came from. A moment before she hadn't known the words, but now, absolutely, still with closed eyes, the girl knew that she was atop a horse, cradled in the arms of its rider.

A man, she thought, and then she knew that word as well.

In the same instant, she knew she was covered by some cloth but naked beneath, and she knew this was a dangerous position in which to find herself.

She had adjusted well enough to the light. She lowered her arm. She opened her eyes.

The sun haloed behind the rider's head. The maiden blinked up at him.

His mouth widened, his teeth flashed.

"Don't," she said, her first word.

"You are safe," the man said. "I rescued you."

He flung his leg over the saddle and slid down, the girl still in his arms. Then he set her, gently, on her feet, and backed away. She was wrapped, she saw, in a rough brown blanket. She had pushed it open when she'd shielded her face from the light, and standing now, she looked down to see her breasts exposed.

The man was an arm's length away, and he kept his gaze on her face. "You are safe," he said again.

The maiden adjusted the blanket so that it covered her more fully. Her questions were many—too many—and they assaulted her all at once. Suddenly her legs were weak and she let them give, collapsing to the ground.

Her hair shifted around her face like a curtain closing, and the girl noticed, with surprise, that it was red.

The man knelt at her side. He reached out as if to touch her, but when she flinched, he drew his hand away.

"Do you know your name?" he asked. "Do you remember what befell you?"

With a mingled sense of shame and regret, the girl shook her head. She remembered nothing.

"I am no one," she said. "I know nothing."

"You are *not* no one," the man told her. "You are the damsel I rescued from a dragon. You are my destiny, and I am yours."

She looked up. His face was open, earnest. Dark curls pulled back from a strong brow; deep-blue eyes, dark like the night sky, were lined with thick, dark lashes. The beginning of a beard, black like his hair. Soft, full lips, parting to reveal a mouth of even, white teeth.

He was smiling, she realized. Not threatening to bite.

"Who are you?" she asked, for though it seemed too much

to hope that he might know who she was, he may, at least, know himself.

"Forgive me," he said. "I am Prince Emory of Harding." He bowed his head formally, and one of his charming curls fell forward, softening his face.

"I saved you," he said again—*Why did he keep saying that?* she wondered— "and I will keep you safe."

The maiden nodded as if she believed him. Did she? Perhaps. It did not matter if she believed him. What she believed would change nothing.

"I need . . . clothing," she said, her cheeks flushing red.

Emory of Harding cleared his throat. "Yes," he said. "It's my regret that I have no gown to offer you. But it would be better than nothing, I am sure," he said, returning to his horse and rifling through his saddlebags, "to wear some things of mine?"

He offered her a white shirt, stale with the smell of his sweat, and a pair of brown breeches. "I wish I had a fur to offer you, as fall chills the air these past nights, but I am in the habit of traveling light. This should suffice, until we reach home. They are not clean, but they are in better repair than what I wear." He gestured to his own black shirt and pants, which, she now saw, were stained both with some sort of white powder and something else, something darker.

Blood.

She took the clothes he offered. "Thank you," she said.

"Of course," he answered. Then his hands went to his waist and he pulled free his belt, and a shock of fear jolted through the place between her legs. But all he did was hand the belt to her. "You will need this more than I do, I suspect."

She took the belt. "Thank you," she said again.

The clothes were ill fitting, of course, but the relief of having her skin covered outweighed the discomfort they caused. She had pulled the waist of the trousers high and wrapped the belt tightly around herself, doubling its knot. The sleeves she'd rolled up to her wrists, and she did her best to ignore the way the shirt smelled and just be grateful for having anything to wear at all.

When she emerged from the thatch of trees where she had dressed, the blanket wrapped around her yet again—for she was cold!—she could remember nothing, but still she felt certain she had never been this cold—she found that Emory had unsaddled the horse and was gathering wood for a fire.

He smiled at her and said, "My clothes look better on you than they do on me," for which she had no answer. Instead of trying to formulate one, she scraped together a pile of browned pine needles to use as kindling.

"The trees are dry enough here that I would normally just use my sword to fell a few branches," Emory said ruefully, "but . . ." He gestured to the belongings he'd pulled from the saddlebags—some dried meat; an empty water bladder; a pair of gloves; a rope; a bag of dust, or sand; a sword, in two pieces, blade and grip.

There was a pickax, as well. "Why not use that?" the girl asked.

"I shall, if need be," Emory answered. "The last time I swung that tool, it was to save my life."

The girl waited, expecting he would say more.

"I nearly fell to my death on my way to save you," Emory said, grinning, and he told the girl about his climb.

"Did we leave the . . . dragon's lair that same way?" she asked when he was done.

"Indeed, we did," Emory answered. "I tied you to my back with that rope and climbed us down, nearly a thousand feet."

The girl searched her memory for any recollection. Surely that was something she would remember. If not her time with the dragon, then being tied naked to a man's back in this freezing cold, descending a thousand-foot cliff that way?

But she remembered nothing. The only sensation was a vague embarrassment upon learning her naked body had been cargo.

"I hope I wasn't too cumbersome" was all she said.

"You're a parcel I'd gladly bear for any distance," Emory answered.

This time, when he smiled, the girl allowed him a small smile in return.

A Woman's Name

By nightfall, the girl had a belly full of fresh-caught rabbit, and a name.

"We shall call you Ama," declared the prince after they had picked the last of the meat from the rabbit's bones, and it seemed a rather rude time to protest, given that this day he had already saved her life, clothed her, and fed her supper.

"A woman's name should begin with an open sound, don't you think?" he continued.

Ama had never thought of it at all, as best she could recollect. "Ama," she repeated. It would do.

The fire warmed them as the sky filled with stars. Nearby, Emory's horse placidly shifted from foot to foot, tail flicking, his lower lip drooping as he slowed and stilled and fell, at last, into a standing sleep.

Ama stared up into the vast brilliance of the stars above and connected them into pictures that only she could see. Emory sat across from her, watching her watch the sky.

She felt nothing. Perhaps somewhere she had, as Emory had, a family waiting for her return. She must. Everyone has people: parents, or siblings, perhaps.

She looked out into the stars and tried to connect them into faces—the faces of the people that might be missing her face, which, she realized, was as a stranger's to her as well.

Abruptly, she said to Emory, "Tell me what I look like."

He started, as if broken from some reverie, and said, "You are lovely, lady, like a flower on a fresh spring day—"

"No," she interrupted. "Stop. Please."

Emory blinked. A moment passed, and then he said, "You have long red hair. It is neither curly nor straight, but somewhere in between. Your skin is pale, almost pink. You're slender. Your breasts—"

"I know all that," Ama interrupted again. "I have seen all that. What I mean to say is, tell me about my face. *That* I haven't seen."

"Oh," said Emory. "Your face." He stared at her as if he was appraising some livestock. "You have light eyes," he began, "not quite yellow, darker than that. Like honey. Better than brown. Quite lovely, even."

"Please," Ama said again. It was quickly becoming her most-used word. "I thank you for your compliments, but if you could just describe me as I am, without flourish or embellishment?"

This request seemed to make Emory uncomfortable, but after a moment he complied. "Your top lip is thinner than your bottom lip," he began, and Ama nodded her encouragement. "Your eyebrows are darker than your hair, more auburn than red." He tilted his head to the side and continued. "Your face isn't round, nor square. Like a cameo, perhaps. And there's pink in your cheeks, but not much. Some meat in your diet, perhaps, that's what you need."

It wasn't a terrible attempt at describing a face, Ama felt, but still she could make no picture from his words. She lifted her hands to her face and felt it. Emory was right about her lips; the bottom did push out farther and softer than the top. Her nose, which he had not mentioned, was thin where it began between her eyes and widened at the nostrils. Still, she found she could not take the parts and make them whole.

Emory stood. "I've an idea," he said. He retrieved the broken blade of his sword. It was, Ama noticed, stained red in some places, dusted with some sort of powder in others. Emory pulled his shirtfront free from the waistband of his pants and set to polishing the steel, wiping away the residue until the metal shone.

"Here," he said, and he placed the blade in Ama's hands.

She blinked down at the reflection there. The blade was too thin to show her countenance all at once, but here was her eye—amber, as Emory had said, flecked with gold—and here was her hairline, red and high, dipping down in the center of her forehead, the skin of which was pinkish-white, as Emory had told her.

There was her nose—a strong nose, not small, and her lips, the top one thin, the bottom full. Her chin, not as sturdy as Emory's, perhaps, but a significant chin, nonetheless.

Ama searched in the parts of her face for something that she could recognize. Something—anything—that would tell her, *this is who you are.*

But there was no recognition. It was a face as unknown to her and as serviceable as her name.

"My thanks," she said, and she returned Emory's blade. There was a stinging in her eyes, and it frightened her, for she knew not what it meant, until water began to brim from them, and then she knew the word for tears.

Emory had but one bedroll, which he laid close to the fire for Ama, and she didn't know if she was supposed to offer to share it with him or not, and so she chose to not. She still had his one rough blanket, too, and that she did offer him, but he refused it.

"What's good enough for Reynard is good enough for me," he said, and he wound the horse's saddle blanket around his shoulders, sat with his back against a nearby tree, legs stretched toward the fire, and said, "You rest, lady. I shall be here when you wake."

Ama lay down on the hard, uncomfortable ground, the thin bedroll barely any padding at all. She turned her face toward the fire and stared into its orange flames, breathing in the waves of heat it threw, hearing from somewhere nearby the call of an owl. "Who? Who?"

And it was with this question ringing in her ears, like a supplication for which she had no response, that Ama fell into a deep and troubled sleep.

Ama's Dream

Luxurious warmth. Liquid warmth. Voluminous warmth.

She stretched her limbs, every joint of them, and she greeted the incalescence that radiated through her body in a powerful wave, in a jolt of welcome lightening.

Above her, huge and heavy in the sky, the red sun smiled down beneficently. She reached up toward it, head back, eyes closed, and lost herself in the wash of its heat.

It warmed her from the outside in, and she felt greedy for more, and more, and more.

She opened her eyes to gaze at her beloved, the sun, and found that it had grown closer. Perhaps she had made it so, with her own desire. It felt powerful enough—her desire—to draw the sun. It filled the whole scope of her vision now, and she could see that the sun was not one bright, flat disc of light, or even a ball of light, but rather a riotous monster of explosive flames.

She was seeing it the way it really was; she was seeing its true red heart aflame and alive. It was her lover, her mate, her first home and her last. It was her own heart made large, and she loved it. She loved the orange-red fuzz of its curve; she loved the roil and boil of its skin; she loved the explosive jets of liquid flame; she loved the quiet dance of whorls and swirls; she loved its glitter and its shine; she loved its movement and its silence. She loved the rivers of plasma, the sprays of flaming crimson, the ribbons of copper, the constantly changing, living, breathing, beating, churning, yearning orb.

She stretched her limbs to reach for it, and there it was. She took it in her hands, reveling in the burn of it. She pressed it to her chest, closed her eyes, rocked it against herself. It was her mother and her child and her lover, too, a trinity undissectible.

She brought it to her face and she kissed it, and then she opened her mouth wide, wider, impossibly wide, and she pushed the sun into her mouth, burning, yes, burning, and she swallowed it down, a path of fire scorching her throat, and then there it was, aflame inside the center of her, alive.

"She's burning with fever," said Emory, so far away as though heard through a long, cold, dark tunnel. "She is too hot to live."

I am finally warm enough, Ama wanted to say, but her mouth was full of fire and she could not speak. Flames melted her eyelids closed and she could not see. The rush of roiling flames inside her made hearing Emory's distant voice nearly impossible.

But she felt herself lifted, and carried, she felt herself jostled and nearly dropped, and then she heard another sound—was it the roar of a beast? The crackle of a fire?

Suddenly, terribly, cold assaulted her. First her feet, her buttocks, the backs of her legs, for she was slung in Emory's arms, and then her knees, her hips, her breasts, her shoulders. She was moaning now, and clinging to him, for he was holding her, still, he was with her in this watery tomb, and she begged him, please, no, anything else, not this, please not this, and she felt the small warmth of his breath against her ear, and she turned toward it, the poor substitute of his human heat better than nothing at all, she turned to his warmth and clung to it, and begged, and then he whispered, "I am so sorry, Ama," and then the cold closed over her, the very top of her head the last part of her to be submerged.

The sun inside her shrunk, closing like a crocus flower in the evening, turning inward, almost gone, almost nothing left at all.

She would die here in the cold. She would die in the wet and the cold, alone except for the arms that encircled her like iron bars.

She fought the cold, she fought the bars, she struggled and thrashed against the horror of it. She would not go like this! She must not!

But her fire was dying, and with it, her will, until, at last, she lay still in the iron maiden of her captor's grip, and she accepted that now she must die.

It was then that her face broke the surface of the water and she gasped, and she coughed and sputtered and choked, and the arms felt not like bars but like buoys, and she clung to them, and she opened her eyes.

Water droplets on her lashes magnified and distorted the light, but there he was, in the rushing river with her, pressing her safe to his chest. He gazed down at her with dark, brilliant blue eyes, eyes not like suns but perhaps like moons. His lips were tinged blue too, drained by the cold river into which he'd thrust them both. Her own trembling fingers reached up to touch his cheek. Rough stubble sandpapered beneath her fingertips.

"I saved you," Emory said.

And Ama believed him.

The King's Steed

They had to take off all their clothes. Soaked clean through, Ama was as frozen as she had been hot in the night. Wildly awake, tremulous with cold, Ama felt her dream leaving her now, quickly, and the orb with it. She clawed at the memory, trying to grasp it, desperate to, but the harder she flung her mind in the direction of the dream the faster it fled, disintegrating like honey in tea until it left nothing but the sweet taste, and then that was gone as well.

There was apparently no time for modesty. Emory stood Ama on her feet near the remaining embers of the fire and stripped her bare, whipping off the belt, the pants slumping to the dirt, yanking the dripping shirt off over her head. Reynard watched with disinterested curiosity as Emory rubbed Ama dry with the coarse wool blanket; he started with her arms, rubbed her breasts, the hard, pink nubs of her nipples, her stomach, her buttocks, the fire of red hair between her legs, her legs themselves.

Her long hair transformed a patch of dirt behind her into mud. She could have wrung the wetness from it, but it was as if she were a baby, unable to care for these things herself. Emory twisted her hair like a rope around his hand and squeezed it from wet to damp. Then he wrapped her tight in the horse blanket, itchy from fur but comforting in its animal smell, and set to drying himself.

Ama watched, arms pinned beneath the blanket, as Emory loosened the shirt ties at the throat and bunched its hem in his hands, pulling it up and over his head. She watched him kick free of his waterlogged boots, as he peeled out of his pants. She saw how the parts of him that were often exposed—his face, his hands, his forearms—were burnished by the sun, but the rest of him was pale—the thick triangular muscles of his legs, his chest, peppered with fine black hairs, and the thick meat of him, a fleshy tusk, white like ivory in the bed of curled black hair.

He saw her watching him, and he stopped, naked, square. He invited her gaze. At last her eyes flicked up to his, and then away. Emory smiled and took up the damp blanket he had used to dry Ama. He rubbed it over his legs and crotch and chest. Then he tied it skirtlike around his waist, threw another few pieces of wood on the embers, and stoked them back to flame.

They had some hot drink, boiled over the fire in a well-used pot pulled from one of Emory's saddlebags. They nibbled dry meat, which Ama found difficult to chew but Emory ripped through easily with his teeth. Reynard was hobbled down by the river so that he could drink and wander a bit, but never far.

As the day warmed and Ama dried, she found herself feeling stronger. The meat did her good, dry and tough though it was; and the drink, bitter and hot, felt as good in the cup between her hands as it did in her stomach.

Emory took care of everything; he brewed the drink, he tended the horse, he handed bite after bite of meat into Ama's hands. He had decided that they would spend this day at rest. Tomorrow would be soon enough to take up their journey.

Ama knew that he was anxious to return to his home, and she was grateful to him for giving her this extra day. She had known him less than two suns, and already she owed him her life twice over! She shuddered to think of what it must have been like before he had come for her—the life she could not remember, when the dragon had ruled her.

Emory had not pressed her memory yet; when she had told him that she could recall naught of that time, he took her at her word. "No need to look back," he said, and she caught a darkness in his expression, which caused her to wonder what terrible things *he* had faced in the dragon's lair, before he smiled again. "We have such a lovely road ahead."

Ama had nodded, but secretly, she did not agree. For what was a person without a past? Was there really nothing behind her? The farthest back she could recall was yesterday, waking on Emory's lap upon Reynard's back, the gentle rocking of the trail.

A life of one day. Ama sipped her drink. Well, that was one thing she knew about herself—she liked this bitter brew.

And another thing: she preferred warmth to cold.

And another: she could not swim.

Emory had laid their clothes out on some rocks in the sun, near the river, to dry. By the time the sun was high above them, the cloth was starting to flap in the breeze. Emory walked down to the boulders and shook out the clothes, turned them.

"If it were summer, these would be dry already," Emory said. "But it is closer to winter than summer now, and the best we can hope for is mostly dry, I think. Our own bodies' heat will have to finish the job." He looked warm enough in just the blanket, Ama thought, and she liked the way his thigh split open the skirt of it when he walked. She liked the whiteness of his legs and the dusky gold of his arms and neck. She liked the loose dark curls around his face. She remembered his ivory tusk and flushed, thinking about it.

To distract herself and disguise what she'd been thinking, Ama said, "Tell me about your horse."

"About Reynard?" Emory looked over at his steed, who looked decidedly un-steed-like right now, his weight heavy on one hip, his long dark tail flicking benignly at imagined flies. "He's a good horse," Emory said, as if that was all there was to know.

"Has he always been yours?" Ama asked.

"As long as he's been alive," Emory answered. "I watched him born six summers past."

"Oh!" said Ama, imagining that. "It must have been special to see such a thing."

"Gory and bloody, it was," Emory answered. "Ridiculous, the size of babies when they slip from their mother's slits." Then he seemed to remember who he was talking to—a lady—for he blustered, "But yes, of course, birth is a miracle."

Ama laughed. The sound of it surprised her, and her eyes widened. The laughter felt good, like a shaft of light.

Emory grinned. "That's the way," he said. And then he continued. "I named him Reynard because I thought it was the kind of name a king's horse should have. I was a grunty lad of twelve, what did I know? But it's a good name, still, I think. A serviceable name."

"Very serviceable," Ama agreed. "And did you train him yourself?"

"Not myself, though I helped," Emory said. "The marshal, Stephen of Harding, he oversees the care and training of all our mounts. But it was well known that I would have Reynard as my horse, as I was coming of age, and as the stallion that fathered him was my father's steed."

"Oh!" said Ama. "Your father? Tell me about him, as well."

"I wish it were that you could know him for yourself, as you will come to know my mother," Emory said, and his voice grew husky, "but he is gone from this world."

"I'm sorry," said Ama. "How very sad for you."

Emory accepted her words with a nod. A moment passed as he steadied his voice and sniffed back what might have become tears.

"He was a good man, a noble man," Emory said finally. "I hope I can step well into the path he forged. With you at my side."

He had said something like that before, when first she came to consciousness in his arms—*You are my destiny, and I am yours.*

Ama did not know how to respond to this; she was not certain what he meant by it, though she suspected. And a little flame in her spurted up—*Do I have no say in this matter?*—but she said nothing of this kind.

Instead she said, "And your father's horse? What of him?"

"He is dead, of course," Emory answered. "The horse goes with the rider."

Ama's eyes went to Reynard, afield by the river, and for a moment it was as if his skin had been flayed back, and there was a skeleton, bones on fire, where the horse should have been.

But then she squeezed her eyes shut, and opened them again, and the horse was there, as he should be, brown pelt dappled in sunlight, placid and perfectly fine.

Ama's Braids

The next morning, when they returned to the road, they sat both astride the horse, Ama in front and Emory pressed behind her, his arms reaching around her sides to hold the reins.

She liked the way he felt, nestled along the length of her body, her head fitting into the nook of his neck, his chest forming a rest upon which for her to lean, each of his legs cupping each of hers. At the small of her back was the waxing and waning of him, sometimes hard, sometimes soft, and either way Ama pretended not to notice.

It was a fine day. The sky, at first just patches of light between trees, widened to a great blue expanse as the day went on and the forest thinned into field. Reynard seemed to have benefited as much from the day of rest as Ama did; he trotted along, knees high, nostrils flared, and he delighted in spooking himself when a squirrel ran across their path.

"Easy," said Emory, but his tone was light; his voice seemed as playful as Reynard's gait.

That morning, before they'd started down the trail, Emory had handed Ama a wide-toothed silver comb she had not noticed before. She liked the way it glinted in the light, and she turned it over in her hands several times, admiring it, until Emory had said, "In case you'd like to arrange your hair," and then Ama realized that she was meant to run it through her tangles.

She had felt her hair and blushed; it was matted from the fever and the river, and it had not occurred to her in the least that it was something she should tend to. But she took the comb and ran it through, picking out the knots, until the teeth no longer caught. Her hair was longer than Emory's; his fell just to his shoulders, though in curls, and hers reached near to her waist.

"May I?" said Emory, and she had nodded, and he had taken her hair in his hands and plaited it into two long braids. "It's a womanish thing to know how to do," Emory admitted, "but when I was a boy my mother allowed me to dress her hair, from time to time." He tied each braid with a piece of leather torn from the piece he used to gather his own hair.

So, when the wind came up on the trail, Ama's hair did not annoy her.

They rode in silence for most of the morning, each enjoying the play of light in the trees and, later, in the tall grasses, when they emerged from the forest. The field in which they found themselves felt almost unreasonably beautiful to Ama; there was so much movement! The way the grasses dipped and swayed as if in waves of green water; the brown and gold birds that flew up out of the grasses, like hidden treasure, when Reynard startled them; the one diamond-backed snake that slithered across their path, emerging suddenly, gazing at them through slit eyes, causing Emory to draw Reynard up short, then disappearing just as quickly into the thick deep grass on the other side of the trail, its skin as shiny as polished wood.

"So much beauty," Ama whispered.

"Yes," Emory agreed, and breathed warmth into her hair, taking a deep breath in as if the smell of her was perfume to him.

"I want to hear about your home," Ama said to Emory after they'd stopped to eat and stretch their legs, when they were back in the saddle once more.

"You'll see it for yourself soon enough," Emory said.

"But as long as we're here," Ama said, "I want to hear how you describe it."

"Well," said Emory, "I'm no bard, but I know my home as well as I know my own horse."

"Good," said Ama. "Tell me."

Emory was quiet for a moment, gathering his thoughts. Then he began, "Harding is probably one of the nicest places you could find. The weather, first off—rarely too cold, only in deep ice a few weeks a year, and the worst of the heat only lasts a month or so in the summer."

"And the people?"

"The people? Oh, everyone is kind. We get along. That is not to say that there are never any problems, but between the castle and the village and the outlying vassals and the servants, we get along better than most."

"Who are your closest companions?" Ama asked.

"Well, I would say my closest friend is the falconer. Pawlin is his name."

"Why him?"

"Why?" Emory said, as if he had never before considered the why of his friendship with the falconer. "Well, we have known each other all our lives. Pawlin was born just six months before I was, and his father often hunted with mine. It made sense for him to be my companion, I suppose." Emory fell quiet for a moment, thinking. Then, just when Ama assumed he had lost that trail of thought, Emory said, "He's funny. I like that about him. He makes me laugh. Oh, he takes everyone to task, Pawlin does! A sharp wit, a quick tongue. Nothing gets past Pawlin. As sharp as Isolda's beak, he is."

"Isolda?"

"His hawk. He's got many birds, an aviary full of them. But Isolda is different than the rest of them."

"Different?"

"Oh, yes. Different."

"How is she different?"

Emory seemed to chew on this question for a good long while. At last he said, "You shall see. Soon enough. You shall."

"And the dragon from which you rescued me?" Ama asked. "What was that creature like? How did you defeat it?"

"Oh," said Emory, "let's not fill your head with such ugly things, when the day is so wide and fine."

And that was all he said about that.

The path they rode parted the tall grass like the hairline on a giant's head. Ama, exhausted still from what had come before, accepted Emory's silence and allowed herself to relax into the arms of her prince. She allowed her neck and eyes to soften, allowed him to hold her there, atop Reynard's back. Emory was steering the way, and Reynard was bearing them forward, and for Ama there was nothing to do but be borne and steered.

The Lynx's Eye

They stopped again well before dark, to make camp one more time. They'd arrive in Harding on the morrow, Emory promised, and the first thing he would do would be to order her a bath—as hot as Ama pleased.

For now, there was no hot water in which to wash, so while Emory unsaddled the horse and cleared a place to build up a fire, Ama wandered away, parting the soft tall grass with gentle hands, stretching her legs and filling her chest with deep breaths.

She didn't plan to go far, for she had no shoes, as Emory's boots were impossibly big, but the ground was even and pleasant, and the whispers of the wind in the grass seemed to promise her something if she walked a bit farther, and then farther still.

Eventually she stopped and turned. She could still see Emory, though he had been shrunk by the distance between them. A reed of smoke rose up from the fire he was building, and Ama felt the pleasure of anticipation of how cozy that would be, to return to a fire, and maybe, even, something warm to drink.

Perhaps that was the trick to living a life, Ama considered, stooping down to admire the purplish tinge at the base of the grasses, the way the color shifted partway up each blade to green and then to caps of gold. Perhaps the key to being content, even without a past, is to keep your eyes firmly on the present moment, and looking no further than what was most probably around just the very next bend—tonight, a fire—and not anticipating beyond that, or allowing oneself to cast backward, into the great black void of before.

Ama heard a rustling sound, and she looked up, kneeling still, disappeared in the grasses. She was not alone.

It was a tremendous kitten, already as large as a small dog, tawny-coated, the promise of black spots not yet fully in, with tall fluffy ears each capped with a pointed tuft of dark hair. It stood just three feet away, short tail at alert, and appraised Ama with its black-lined saffron eyes.

"Oh," Ama said. "Hello."

The kitten did not seem to fear her in the least. When Ama stretched out her hand, the kitten stepped forward to smell it. Its soft whiskers tickled her palm; its dry dark nose snuffled around, and then its tongue emerged, rough and pink, to kiss her or to taste her, Ama didn't know, but she was delighted.

"You are a darling," she said to the kitten, who allowed her to pet its head. A rumbling sound erupted from the kitten's chest—a purr.

Another rustle. Another cat emerged—this one, the mother. She was enormous. From where Ama crouched, her hand still on the kitten's head, she found herself looking up as if in prayer at the mother cat's chest. Thick white fur radiated out, all white from neck to belly, and down the insides of her legs, as well. Her massive paws—as big as Ama's feet—flattened the grass beneath them.

The cat's expression was all danger—narrowed eyes, turned-back tufted ears, bared teeth. A sound rumbled in her chest too, but not a purr. A growl.

"Oh," said Ama again.

She stayed perfectly still, facing the cat but not staring right into her eyes, keeping her gaze respectfully lowered. Slowly, slowly, she withdrew her hand from the lynx's kitten.

She placed her hands on the ground in supplication. And though she did not speak, she told the lynx, with every hair on her head, every inch of her flesh, *I respect you. I honor you. I leave you in peace.*

Perhaps the mother lynx understood, for her ears, which had been pinned back, rotated forward as if she were listening, and her black lips softened around her teeth.

The kitten purred more loudly and stepped forward, butting Ama's arm with its head, as if trying to get her to pet it again. Ama ignored its advances, silently willing it to return to its mother's side.

It wasn't long before the kitten abandoned its pursuit of Ama's affection. It turned its short tail to her and went to its mother, weaving between her legs.

The mother cat, with her babe returned to her, looked now at Ama with something akin to curiosity. She tilted her head to the side and widened her eyes, and her gaze seemed to ask, *What are you doing here?*

It was a fair question, Ama thought. She would have liked to have known the answer herself.

Ama's gaze, which she'd held low in deference, glanced up to meet the lynx's eyes. They were milky jade with infinitely black ovular pupils—not round, like Emory's, not horizontal, like Reynard's, not slitted, like the snake's. The top and bottom of each pupil was tipped into a point. And, with a startled shiver of something like memory, Ama felt certain she had seen eyes like these before.

It was right there—in the back of her brain, in the shine of the mother cat's eyes—a recollection, a calling back, a cognizance. If the cat would hold perfectly still. If she could move an inch closer. If they could gaze a moment longer, then, Ama felt certain, she could remember.

Her fingers twitched with their desire to grab on to whatever it was her mind was reaching for, spinning for, even as it frightened her. Around them, around the mother and the kitten and Ama, the wind stirred the grasses in a whirl. The clouds overhead glowed red as the setting sun sang out the last and loudest of its day, the sky growing velvet as it darkened.

Ah, there was beauty all around—in the purple stalks of the dancing grass, in the wide and wild sky, in this creature's eyes, as she stood still, trying, Ama was sure, to tell her something.

And then something flew at them, not a bird, no, not a bird, and the lynx's eyes shifted, too late, away from Ama's, and Emory's pickax struck the scruff of white at her throat.

Ama screamed as the lynx fell, wet with blood, into the now still grass, and the kitten cried piteously for its mother.

Ama's Sorrow

"What have you done?" Ama said, her voice barely a scratch, so tight was her throat. The mewling kitten was pacing back and forth in front of its dead mother's face. Blank now, the eyes held no secrets.

"I've saved your life again," said Emory, reaching down for his weapon and jerking it free, dropping it with a thud into the grass. Blood poured from the wound, thickened, stopped. "It's becoming quite a habit of mine, it seems."

He turned to the kitten, grabbed it by its scruff, and hefted it into the air. "A shame about the kit, but nothing for it but to make it quick," he said, and as he moved his hands, Ama saw with a flash what he planned to do—a quick jerk, a broken neck, the babe dead beside its mother.

"No!" she screamed, tripping wildly to her feet, grabbing for the animal in his arms. "No, you can't!"

Emory stopped and smiled down at Ama as if she were an over-tired child. "Dear girl," he said, "I must. There's no chance for a kit on its own. It would be cruel to let it wander and starve."

"Please," said Ama, knowing, somehow, that this was the right way to get what she needed. She made herself seem small and turned her hands palms-up, in supplication rather than demand. "Please, give it to me. Let me keep it as a pet."

Emory looked as if he might relent, though he said, "Animals like this don't make for pets, Ama. Better to let Mother give you one of her cats, if you like, when we reach the castle. She's like you, in that way. Crazy for cats."

"No," said Ama, but it came out too strong, she could tell, by the way Emory's face closed to her. She tried again. "Please," she began, for he had liked that word. "Please. Perhaps the cat can keep me warm. When you are not able to."

This brought a smile to Emory's lips. And then he extended his arms, passing the kitten, who yowled and clawed and would have cried if its eyes knew how, into Ama's grasp.

"You shall have to learn for yourself, I suppose," he said grudgingly, "that wild beasts are not meant to be tamed."

Ama curled the cat into her arms, and she wanted to turn her back to Emory, she wanted to march away, but instead she looked up at him through tear-bright lashes and said, "Thank you."

❁❁❁

It was a long and terrible night. The kitten, forlorn, screamed and yowled. It seemed that she would never stop—Ama had learned that the kitten was a female—and Ama's chest and hands were striped bloody from its claws. But she would not let go, she would not release the kitten to the black night and the dangers that would consume it, were she not to hold on. Every yowl, every scratch, Ama took without complaint, for she knew it was her fault that this kitten had no mother. She had held the mother cat's gaze too long; Ama had allowed the hunter to catch the lynx unaware.

At last, at last, the kitten collapsed against her and slept, crying small piteous cries in its restless sleep.

Ama did not sleep. She lay along the fire, pressed the kitten to her heart, and made promises all the night long: promises to the kitten, to the kitten's lost mother, to the hard, hot anger in her own breast.

By morning, she managed to tuck away the anger, as the kitten seemed to tuck away its grief. The kitten drank the fresh water Emory brought up from the stream and ate Ama's breakfast of dried meat.

Emory had gutted and skinned the lynx the night before, but Ama would not eat a bite of it. She refused too the hot brew Emory offered her with sunup, saying that her stomach felt unsettled, and drinking only water.

Emory packed the saddlebags a final time, flung the lynx's skin across Reynard's back, and offered Ama a hand into the saddle.

She shook her head, tucked the kitten more firmly into her shirtfront, and said, "I shall walk, if it pleases you. My legs are restless from yesterday's long ride."

"It does not please me," Emory said. "With no food in you last night or this day, and weak still from your fever? You should ride."

Ama said nothing.

Emory sighed. Perhaps he understood that Ama would not ride with the kitten upon his mount, with the lynx's fur as well.

"As you say," he said, but he would not ride either, so they walked off together, Reynard pleased to bear only the weight of the saddlebags and the pelt, Emory with the reins in his hand, and Ama with the kitten in her shirt.

"What shall you call it?" Emory asked.

"Sorrow," Ama answered, which she had named the kitten, deep in the night, when Emory and Reynard had slept. It was a word she had not known until she thought it. And she wished there were another, sweeter thing to call the kitten, but better honesty than lies.

"That's an awful name for a pet," Emory said bluntly.

"Yes," said Ama. "Reynard is a much more agreeable name. But her name is Sorrow, just the same."

And so it was that Emory of Harding returned home, a dragon slayer and a king, with a lynx skin to give his mother, a damsel to take as his bride, and Sorrow, who would remain his bride's companion as long as she remained at his side.

THREE

Harding's Wall

The sun was setting when Emory and Ama arrived at the wall of Harding.

From the distant hill where Emory told Reynard "whoa," and the horse stopped and stomped his foot, Ama took in her first view of the place that she was to henceforth call home. Below them, in a valley and beyond, lay the expanse of Harding. Ama could see the smart configuration of buildings, which had been built in a labyrinthine pattern around a central castle—Emory's castle.

The castle was by far the largest structure, and the city circled it like an iris around a pupil. It was a miracle of turrets and garrets, of pinnacles and parapets. And the whole of it was built of some stone of lustrous black, so it gleamed like an iris, as well.

The lesser buildings were constructed of lesser stones—dull shades of brown and gray and mud. And surrounding all of it was the wall of Harding.

The wall stretched, almond-shaped, around the city. And it seemed to catch and reflect the last of the day's sun, a million points of light sparkling from its surface.

"Home at last," Emory sighed contentedly. He turned and smiled at Ama, and the brilliant wide happiness reflected there lifted Ama's heart, in turn, and she felt a surge of hope, and she felt her own mouth smile in return.

Reynard knew where they were, and what that meant—a return to his comfortable stable, oats instead of grass, a bedful of wood shavings, fresh fruit. He snorted happily and tossed his head, and, but for Emory's hand on his reins, would have finished the journey at a gallop.

But, still on foot beside his mount, Emory controlled him, and side by side, Emory, Reynard, and Ama approached the wall, with Sorrow still tucked to her breast.

Down the hill they went, and across the last flatness of plain, and then there they were, at the foot of the wall, which cast them deep into shadow.

The wall was full of eyes—unblinking, steadfast, watching eyes. It was the eyes that had caught the light and glinted it up at her; they were everywhere, mortared into the wall's surface—eyes of every shade of blue and gray and green and brown.

Everywhere, everywhere, eyes.

"It's a sight, isn't it?" Emory said, seemingly unaware of his wordplay. "Harding is known throughout the world for its wall."

"But," said Ama, clutching the sleeping lynx tighter, "whose eyes are those?"

"Those are the Eyes of Harding," Emory said. "They are made by our glassblower—the finest in the world, I might add. He alone crafts the Eyes for our wall. His gaze is our gaze, and the Eyes never blink, never rest, as they guard our border. Those who live behind the wall know we are safer for their watchful protection."

Ama reached out a hand and stroked the wall—the rough stones, the sandy mortar, the cool, smooth glass Eyes, one after another after another, all unblinking.

Now, close up, she saw that here and there, an Eye was missing—not many, but a few distinct pits where Eyes had been and were no more.

She ran her fingers inside one such groove, felt the absence there.

"They are considered prizes beyond measure," Emory said. "The Eyes of Harding are said to bestow fortune upon he who possesses them. Only the glassblower can form them. He crafts other pieces, as well; his intricate and beautiful creations can be found in the finest estates all across this wide world, fetching any price he chooses to set, so well known and respected he is, but the Eyes are a different matter. The glassblower makes them only for the wall of Harding. And, of course, it should go without saying that no one may take an Eye from the wall. Still," Emory conceded, "it happens from time to time. A desperate soul, out of hope, out of options—perhaps a man whose wife is dying, or someone who has lost all his wealth in a bad bet—occasionally such a bereft creature will venture to the wall and scoop an Eye from it."

"Does it work?" Ama asked. "Will an Eye give its bearer luck?"

"Some say it does," said Emory. "But always, the thief is caught."

"What then?"

"We are not a cruel people, Ama," Emory said. "But we are fair. The law of Harding dictates: An eye for an Eye."

Ama shivered. The sun was gone now; the Eyes did not shine; the lynx kit mewled for her supper.

A great wooden door was set into the wall, a third the height of the wall itself. Dark ironwork slashed across it, reinforcing it against intruders. At its center was an enormous golden knocker, shaped into the head of a dragon.

Emory reached up and grabbed the ring that hung from the dragon's jaws and clanged it, hard, against the brass plate beneath it.

A moment passed, and Ama heard the turning of a lock before a small window opened just beneath the dragon knocker. A face—sharp-featured, white-skinned, scarred—peered out.

The gatekeeper's eyes widened. "Prince Emory!" he said.

Emory flourished a hand in Ama's direction, and she imagined how she must appear—day-old braids falling into tangles, dirt-stiffened men's clothing, a wildcat's face peering out from her shirt.

Emory said, "I left as a prince. I return as king."

The gatekeeper's eyes flashed over Ama and then, with deference, away. "My king," he said, and then he slammed shut the small opening.

Moments later the great door swung, preceded by a clattering of bars and locks. The gatekeeper, no taller than a child, and wispy as the grasses in the field where Ama had found Sorrow, bowed low, his face brushing his own knees. "My king," he said again, and then, angling his bow in Ama's direction, "My queen-in-waiting."

Ama bowed her head in return, which seemed to flummox the gatekeeper, who bowed even lower, to which Ama nodded her head again, which prompted the gatekeeper to bow so low that Ama feared he may snap in half, so she raised her chin this time instead of lowering it, which seemed to please the gatekeeper, who returned to standing.

"Welcome home," he said, and stood to the side, gesturing for them to precede him through the gate and into Harding.

Ama's Bath

Stepping through the gate, hearing it thud closed behind them, was but the first step to the castle. From the hill, Ama had seen the vast labyrinth of structures that surrounded Emory's home, and the cobbled roads that twisted between them proved as circuitous as they had seemed from outside.

Emory had handed the lynx pelt to the gatekeeper, who promised it would be delivered to the queen, and then he reseated Ama, and the lynx kit with her, atop Reynard. Emory mounted himself behind Ama, and he prodded Reynard with his heels. Reynard, eager to get home to bed and oats, obligingly trotted forward.

Everywhere, faces peered out at them—at their returning king, yes, but, Ama knew, at her, as well, the stranger Emory had brought home with him, like a souvenir from a strange land.

The farther they traveled into the heart of the village, the more the sensation of being a thing on display intensified, for everywhere eyes were upon her—from the open windows and doorways of thatched-roof village homes; from market stands, as customers and vendors alike stretched their necks in her direction; from the faces of beggar children, following behind Reynard until Ama voiced her concern that the children would get lost, this far away from their parents, and Emory told them, gruffly, to be on their way.

Hands reached out to touch Reynard's coat, Emory's boot, Ama's bare foot. She wanted to be like Sorrow, who had pulled her head down into Ama's shirt; she wanted to tuck herself away inside of someone else, to disappear. And so she hunched back into Emory's arms, was grateful that he was steering the way and not she; she closed her eyes for minutes at a time, reopening them only to check their progress to the castle, willing herself to be numb, invisible.

At last they reached the magnificent central structure, which had its own walls, these made, as was the castle itself, of glossy black stone. It was dark by the time they arrived there, and lit torches cast their orange reflections all along the parapets. Where the torch-light did not reach, the castle walls fell into inky shadow.

Inside the castle wall, Emory dismounted, helped Ama down, and handed Reynard's reins to a waiting boy. He slapped the horse's haunch, said "Well done" to the horse and "Treat him well" to the boy.

Ama was sorry to see Reynard's hind end walking away from

her, but she did not have time to think long on it, for a bouquet of ladies descended upon them, curtsying and giggling, and they surrounded Ama. Sorrow poked her head out of Ama's neckline, saw the crowd of girls, and hissed her displeasure.

A girl in a pink dress squealed with fright, and several others collapsed into laughter upon finding that their queen-in-waiting had a wildcat in her shirt.

"Enough, enough," Emory scowled, and the twittering and giggling trailed off and stopped.

"My queen," Emory said, with a formal bow to Ama, "I deliver you to your ladies, who will take you to your room and see you washed and dressed."

Panic sent Ama's heart racing. "You are leaving me?" she said. "Please, do not leave me."

"Dear heart," Emory said, his mouth spreading in a handsome grin, "we shall be together again soon. Grant me leave so that I may return to you smelling and looking fresh, as you deserve me."

At this, the bevy of ladies were set atwitter once more, and there was nothing for Ama to do but drop a clumsy curtsy, one hand clutching Sorrow, the other waving aimlessly at her side, as she had no skirt.

Then Emory bowed again, and, flanked by men who Ama had not noticed before, he took his leave of her, giving Ama to the women.

***

The castle was cold. So much stone, such high ceilings. Ama, surrounded by the ladies, made her way through the front hall, up one staircase, down another long passage, and up a second set of stairs. Soon she lost all sense of where she was, the route through the castle as labyrinthine as the road through the village of Harding had been.

There were too many branching hallways for Ama to keep track, and doorways, some yawning open, others shuttered closed by iron-girded doors; there were tapestries on the walls that seemed to tell stories—down this hall, a series of hangings that depicted men in armor, astride horses, lances in hand, meeting in battle, and, in the final hanging, just before the corridor turned, one of the knights skewered by the other's weapon, red petaling out from his back, his iron-helmeted head slumped sideways.

Up a short flight of stairs and down the long stretch of the next hall, Ama slowly passed another tapestry story: this one began with a man on a horse, alone, a bright-orange sun woven into the background. It could have been any noble-born man; the horse, dappled gray and high-hooved, pranced up a gilded road, and the man was dressed in finery, chin high, cheeks red with health. The progression of wall hangings showed his route down the road, as the sun set behind him and the full moon rose in its place, and as the seasons shifted, too, from golden summer to frosty winter. Nothing happened, really, in these images; though the world around him transformed from day to night and summer to winter, the man himself remained steadfast in his seat, the same cunning smile on his face, the same knowing gaze in his eyes.

As they made their way deep into the castle, Ama abandoned herself to the twittering girls, nodding agreement and laughing when it seemed called for, giving them the little information she could about who she was—all information that Emory had given her.

Her name? Ama.

Where she came from? Emory had rescued her from a dragon in a gray land.

Before that? She did not know.

Her people? She knew not if she had people, save Emory himself.

Her pet? A lynx called Sorrow.

Ama could not track how long they walked or make sense of the deep route they took into the stone heart of the castle. Time was lost to her, and distance. With each turn they took, each step they paced, Ama felt her own heart constrict, as if the iron and the stone of the castle seized and squeezed it tight.

At last they stopped in front of a chamber door. One of the girls pushed it open, then stood aside and curtsied so that Ama could enter first. With Sorrow still tucked into her shirt, Ama passed across the threshold and into the large stone room.

Already a great heat emanated from the fireplace, the crackle and hum of the flames the friendliest sound Ama had yet heard.

Across the room was a high curtained bed, layered in fabrics and furs.

As Ama stood surveying her room, a dozen girls poured in behind her, each in a dark dress with white aprons over, bringing pot after pot of hot water, with which they filled a round deep tub. Someone else brought water for the lynx and a slice of meat as well and set the food and drink in a corner. Ama set Sorrow in front of the food, but the kitten would not eat it at first, skulking around the room's perimeter, hackles raised, as if searching for a way out. But the door was closed tight to keep in the heat from the fire that was built up high, and to keep out prying eyes, and after circling the room, Sorrow set in to eat the meat.

A girl in a coarse gray gown, who told Ama to call her Tillie, reached to pull Ama's tunic over her head. Ama allowed it, lifting her arms as if she were a child. Then Tillie pulled loose the knot in Emory's leather belt, and the girls twittered to think of Emory riding all those miles with no belt around his waist, and imagining how it must have been when he found Ama in the lair, when she had been naked in his arms, for somehow they had heard already the roughest details of Ama's rescue.

"'Tain't every day we have a story such as yours," Tillie said, a wide immodest grin on her young, pale, freckled face. "It's like a fairy story, that's what it is."

Then Ama was naked, and all the girls averted their eyes as not to be caught staring, but of course they all snuck glances, one and then another, and they made their judgments.

At last Ama stepped into the tub and sunk down into the steaming water, the muscles in her shoulders, her back, her buttocks, her legs relaxing and unwinding, muscles she hadn't realized she'd held tensely, and she let Tillie unweave her tangled hair and soak it in the water, and she closed her eyes and filled her chest with air.

She breathed, and she settled into the bath, and she felt, though not at home, at least warmed through. Opening her eyes, she saw Sorrow sitting prettily in front of the fire, licking her whiskers and cleaning her face with her paw.

The Queen's Gift

Ama did not want to ever leave her bath, but water does not remain warm forever, and too soon staying in the bath felt a less comfortable option than rising from it.

Tillie was there to receive her with a length of white linen, which she rubbed all over Ama's body to dry her in front of the fire. Ama lifted her arms and Tillie rubbed dry the twin thatches of red hair there, as well as the matching thatch lower, between Ama's legs.

Tillie squeezed Ama's hair until it no longer dripped, and she wrapped it in another length of linen before she set to dressing Ama.

First came the underdressing—loose breeches, with a slit at the crotch, and a long plain chemise that fell from Ama's shoulders to her ankles, with sleeves ending at her wrists. The underdressing fit well, but not perfectly, and as Tillie adjusted Ama into it, she called out notes to another girl whom she called Rohesia, this one dressed in blue: "We'll need to add a half inch to the hem," she said, "and take in the bust a bit. The sleeves are fine for this style, but for the other gown, with loose sleeves, we shall add an inch."

Rohesia took notes in a leather-bound notebook, which she pulled from a pouch at her waist, scribbling with a graphite rod.

Sorrow had curled into a ball on a deerskin rug just at Ama's feet, by the fire, and she, at least, looked content in this new home.

Underdressing settled, Tillie regarded the two dresses laid across the tall canopied bed. "I think the green is a color better suited to your hair," she said, talking more to herself than Ama. "But the queen mother sent up the red dress just this morning, from her own wardrobe." She pulled the linen from Ama's hair and held the dress up next to it, considering.

"It is perhaps more important to please the queen mother with the red than the king with the green," she said. "It is clear that the king is already pleased with you, even in men's breeches."

As Tillie and Rohesia lowered the dress over Ama's head and fastened its buttons and stays, Ama made herself compliant. The fire blazed up red, and Ama stared into it with greedy eyes. The flush of heat on her face, the brilliance of its movement and its colors—red, yes, but orange, too, and yellow, and purplish-blue at the base of the flames—all of it together set Ama's head to peace, and she felt as though she could stay just there, forever, even more willingly than in the bath, for it was this dry heat and the liveliness of the flame that she craved.

Then Tillie rotated her again, and Ama found herself in a tall, ovular mirror. There, at her feet, slept Sorrow. The dress, dark-red velvet, trimmed with white fur at the wrists and neckline. Hair, still damp, falling near to her waist and glowing red in the fire's light.

"You are lovely," said Tillie, and her voice held no jealousy, and no admiration, either. It was a statement of fact, no more. "Now, to tend to your hair."

The only request Ama made was that they move a chair for her in front of the fire, rather than leaving its warmth to fashion her hair. Other than that, she left the decisions to Tillie—where to braid, what to leave loose, whether to place a circlet upon her head or leave her hair, as Tillie said, "devastatingly bare."

Tillie chose a network of braids, some thick, some narrow, and she looped and pinned them across Ama's head, tucking their ends under and pinning them at the nape of her neck.

By the time she had finished, it had been dark for several hours, and the tall canopied bed, draped with furs, seemed to call out to Ama. Oh, she was tired!

But there would be no rest for her, not now, not soon, for Tillie said, "The queen mother and the king await you in the great hall, my lady."

She knelt at Ama's feet, holding satin slippers for Ama to step into, and then she stood, flattening her dress with her hands, and regarded Ama as one would regard a well-prepared meal or a finely arranged bunch of flowers.

"You should please," she said, and then she dropped a pretty curtsy and turned to go.

"Wait!" Ama called. "If I am to go to the great hall, who shall stay with Sorrow?"

"The cat?" Tillie asked. "She will be fine here, on her own. She has eaten, now she sleeps."

"She has not been alone since parted from her mother," Ama said. "And this is her first night in a strange room, and under a roof of any kind. It would set my mind to ease, knowing she was not left here on her own."

"She is but a pet," Tillie said, but then perhaps she saw something in Ama's expression, for she lowered her head and said, "I myself will stay with your Sorrow."

"My thanks," Ama said, grasping Tillie's hand in hers. "I will remember your kindness."

"It is my pleasure to serve my queen-in-waiting," Tillie said with another curtsy.

Ama almost curtsied in return, but then she remembered the confusion of the gatekeeper, and so she did not, instead raising her chin as a queen might do and turning to the door, careful with her skirts not to disturb the sleeping lynx.

Ama's Stories

Rohesia led Ama through the maze of the castle, and Ama wondered, winding down yet another hallway, how long it would take her to untangle the architectural riddles of this place.

At last they came to the great hall, which glowed in candlelight; a vast black iron chandelier hung above the expansive wooden table, bare except for candles.

The candles above and below dipped and swayed, throwing shadows on the walls around. Sitting at the table, just to the right of its head, was the queen mother. Like Ama, she was dressed in red, though her hair was perhaps more suited for the color, jet-black as it was, with streaks of white at the temples.

And at her elbow stood Emory, clean now, and dressed in finery, but with the same easy white smile, the same dark curls, washed and worn loose. He was tall and fine and cut a handsome figure standing there, waiting for Ama. At the sight of him, Ama felt her mouth part into a smile, for it was a relief to see his familiar face in this strange place, and the way his eyes lit up with pleasure upon seeing her made Ama feel glad for the care Tillie had taken with her gown and hair.

"Ama," he said upon her entrance. "What a sight you are!"

He strode across the hall and took up Ama's hands, kissing them both, one and then the other.

He smelled better, too, Ama noticed.

"Hello," she said, and dropped a curtsy, one quite better than her earlier attempts. She seemed to be a quick study, Ama thought about herself.

"And you've put aside your cat," Emory said, sounding particularly pleased.

"Only just for dinner," Ama corrected. "Tillie—one of the girls who tended to me—is with her."

Emory laughed loud at this. "Did you hear that, Mother?" he said. "A nursemaid for her cat!"

"I would do the same for my favorite pets," the queen mother said. "It is no surprise at all, to me."

Still holding Ama by a hand, Emory led her across the hall and to the table. There, he presented her to his mother. "May I present the lady Ama," he said formally, "the damsel I have rescued from the dragon I conquered, in a land far away and gray as dusk."

But dusk wasn't gray, Ama thought. Dusk was the most colorful hour, with the horizon set on fire by the breath of the yawning sun. She did not say this, however. She had better sense than that, and instead dropped another curtsy, this time bowing deep and lowering her gaze, as well. "Queen Mother," she said. "Thank you for the lovely gown. I hope you are pleased by how it looks on its grateful recipient."

"Come closer, girl," the queen mother said, and Ama obeyed. Emory dropped her hand and she walked alone to the queen mother's side.

"Look at me," the queen mother said, and Ama did. The queen mother looked back, and each studied the other.

Ama did not know what the queen mother saw, but in the queen mother's face, Ama saw gray cliffs and bright clusters of jewels and steamed-over rose-gold mirrors.

Then she blinked hard, and looked again, and she saw an elegant matron, still beautiful, with black eyes and thin pale lips, her face all eye and eyebrow and forehead and hair.

Ama curtsied again.

"Enough of that," the queen mother said, and gestured to the chair across from her, at Emory's left hand. "Sit," she said, and Ama sat.

The queen mother snapped her fingers, and the servants, whom Ama had not noticed, came alive, pouring wine into goblets, trimming the candle wicks along the table's spine. Another servant, this one a girl no older than Ama, uncovered the dishes lining a side table, and a tall, dour-faced man, candle-like both in the waxiness of his features and the long, thin shape of him, brought the first dish to the table.

"May I serve their majesties?" he asked.

"Serve the ladies first," Emory told him.

The candle man bowed his head and did as he was ordered, laying a slice of meat first on the queen mother's silver plate and then another slice on Ama's.

A parade of servants came to the table, each adding a portion of another dish to Ama's plate. She watched the food pile in front of her until, at last, they stopped.

There was so much food on the plate that Ama felt slightly ill just looking at it, so instead of eating, she raised her goblet and sipped the wine, which warmed her throat and then her chest with each swallow.

"Slowly," Emory warned kindly, "or you will regret it on the morrow."

They ate. It was a long, wide table for just the three of them to sit, and as Ama gazed at all the vast, empty space, all the unseated chairs, Emory said, "Tomorrow the hall will be full, as it usually is, but this is your first night in the castle, and Mother desired to have you all to ourselves."

"When the rest of the court gets their claws into you," the queen mother said, a piece of meat on her fork, "they may never let go. Better we speak first and learn what you know of yourself, before they try to wrest it from you."

"I told you, Mother," Emory said, with an air of exasperation, as if he'd already explained this to her several times, "Ama knows nothing of her time before her rescue."

"Do not begrudge me the chance to hear from the girl herself," the queen mother said to Emory, and then, to Ama, "Well?"

Ama swallowed. "Well, what?" she said loudly.

It was impertinent, and unexpected, and perhaps brought on by the quick draught of wine, but as soon as the words were out, Ama wished she could call them back.

It was as if a window had blown open and brought inside a freezing draft, icing everyone into stillness. The servants stopped where they stood, Emory paused midbite. Even the candles seemed to cease their flicker.

And then the queen mother laughed—a loud, triumphant sound, warmer than Ama would have guessed her capable of.

"Cheeky!" she said, and lifted her goblet, raised it in Ama's direction. "I like that." She drank deeply and set her cup back down with a clatter. "*Well,*" she started again. "What do you remember of your time in the dragon's possession, and the time before that, child?"

Ama cast herself back, back, back. There were colors. And there was light. And warmth—oh, such lovely warmth.

But that was all there was.

Now, there was this—this man who had rescued her, who looked after her with such gentle attentiveness, this queen mother with the audacious, wonderful laugh. Here, food, more than enough food, and pleasant drink. Warm clothes. Upstairs, her lynx. A warm bed, waiting for her. A fire, all her own, in a room, all her own.

It was enough, Ama thought. It would have to be.

"I remember nothing," she told the queen mother. "I will need new stories, I suppose."

"Then, my dear," the queen mother said, "we shall help you to make them."

And she raised her goblet once more, and Ama raised hers, and Emory, too, raised his. The queen mother said, "To new stories," and their three goblets met with a clang, and together, they drank to the future.

When the dinner dishes were removed and a spread of sweets was set before them, the queen mother addressed the question Ama had been silently harboring, as if she intuited that a bit of sugar would help Ama swallow what was to come.

"Now," the queen mother said, spearing a sugared berry as she spoke, "we have a wedding to plan."

Ama too had a selection of delicacies on her gilded plate, but she set her fork quietly down and folded her hands in her lap.

"And before the wedding, the coronation," Emory said. "I have, after all, returned home with a damsel, having felled a dragon."

"Indeed, my son," the queen mother said. "You are a king, that is certain, and we must waste no time in announcing it. After all, it has been more than a month since the last king has left this world, and the people deserve to know that Harding is under the protection of a new one. The arrangements have been made already, Emory, for the morrow."

At this, Emory's eyes widened. "You arranged the coronation ceremony in my absence?"

"Of course," the queen mother said.

"But if I hadn't returned—"

"That is not a thought a mother entertains," interrupted the queen mother, as if even the idea of Emory failing to return to the castle was too bitter to consider. "You returned home to Harding as king, having earned your position as tradition dictates, and you shall be celebrated as such, without delay."

Emory reached across and took his mother's hand, squeezed it. Ama watched as mother and son shared a deep, long gaze, each one's love for the other writ clear upon their faces.

She was, Ama felt, both at the table and entirely invisible. It was through Emory's rescue of her from the dragon that he was now to be crowned king, but in this moment Ama wondered if she could have been anyone, anyone at all, and the plates spread on the table would still be heavy with the same sugared fruits and dishes of cream.

Ama was, she saw, both terrifically important and terribly insignificant, in equal measures, at exactly the same time.

When she looked up from her plate, it was to find that the queen mother had shifted her gaze from Emory to Ama; gone was the gentle gaze of mother love, replaced by something else. Something sharper.

"Dear girl," the queen mother said. "Tomorrow you shall see our Emory crowned king, and in less than two months, at midwinter solstice, you shall become his queen. What do you think of that?"

"It is a wonder," said Ama. "Truly, it is."

"Indeed," said the queen mother, and she picked up her glass goblet by its delicate stem. She held it before a candle and twirled it, gazing into the glistening red wine. "It is dizzying, the wonder of it all." She brought the goblet to her lips and drained it. A servant was at her elbow before the cup had reached the table, and he poured another long stream of wine.

"I do hope, though," Ama said, choosing her words carefully, "that perhaps some search can be made for my family? So they might know of my fate?"

Emory cleared his throat as if to speak, but the queen mother laid her hand on his arm.

"Your family?" said the queen mother.

"Well," said Ama, "there must be *someone*, after all. That is to say, everyone comes from a mother and a father, do they not? Surely someone, somewhere, is anxious to hear of my safe escape from the dragon, just as you were anxious to see your son safely home."

"Dear girl," said the queen mother firmly. "You have no family."

"No family?" Ama said, her throat closing. "Why do you say that?"

"The dragons, they do not . . . take girls with families." The queen mother's face was gentle, sympathetic. "Emory didn't tell you?"

Ama shook her head.

"He should have," the queen mother said, frowning briefly at her son, "so that you wouldn't have false hopes. It is kinder that way."

"It is true, Ama," Emory said now, leaning in toward Ama. "The damsel never has kin. It is known."

"By whom?" Ama asked, but she felt in her bones the truth of his words.

"By all," said the queen mother, as if that settled the matter. And it did.

"But we shall be your people," Emory said, and he laid his warm hand gently atop Ama's. As he did, servants appeared with still more food, laying a plate of ripe plums before them.

"In seven weeks' time, my son shall be your husband, and he shall give you a son; that is all the family you should need," the queen mother said.

"Seven weeks," Emory echoed, picking up a plum and, with a burst of juice, biting into its red flesh. "Seven weeks to learn the ways of Harding, the ways of the castle, and the ways of a queen."

Seven weeks, then, before the year's shortest day, the year's longest night. Ama's throat felt tight and dry. She lifted her glass—such a lovely glass, she noticed—and drained it.

Ama's Visitor

It was well past midnight when Ama was returned to her room. Tillie was there, as she had promised, sitting in the chair where Ama had sat for the styling of her hair.

Perhaps Tillie had been asleep, for when Ama entered, led by Rohesia, she stood quickly, as if startled into wakefulness.

The lynx lay, still curled, on the hearthrug, and Ama's entrance did not disturb her in the least. Ama noticed that someone had fetched a box of sand and placed it in a corner, for Sorrow to use.

"My lady," said Tillie, dropping into a curtsy.

"Thank you for staying with Sorrow," Ama said. "I rested easy knowing she was in your care."

"Pay it no concern, my lady," Tillie said, though now Ama wondered if Tillie had missed her supper because of the assignment. But when she asked, Tillie shook her head and said, "It's kind of you to worry, but I have no needs."

Ama thought it was an odd way of saying that she was not hungry.

Then Rohesia set to building up the fire, and Sorrow stirred at the new warmth of it, stretching her legs and yawning, her sharp kitten teeth white against the pinkness of her tongue.

Tillie helped Ama out of her gown and underdressing and into a thin pale chemise. She took down Ama's hair and arranged it in a simple plait, then turned back the covers and the furs for Ama to climb into bed.

Oh, such luxury, to climb into a warm bed, heated by stones tucked between the sheets. Oh, such luxury, to rest her head on the bolster, to watch Tillie unfasten and close the curtains of the canopy.

Sorrow leaped prettily to the foot of the bed just before Tillie lowered the final curtain, and she said crossly, "Out of the mistress's bed, you beast." But Ama reached out and stroked the cat.

"Leave her," she said, and Tillie pursed her mouth as if she wanted to argue, but here in her chamber it was clear that Ama was in charge, and so Tillie did not protest.

"Sweet dreams, lady," she said, dropping the curtain and leaving the room.

Ama was alone for the first time since . . . well, since *ever,* as far as time mattered. With no memories of *before,* all Ama had were the days with Emory and this evening, at the castle. To be by herself, in a safe and comfortable bed, with only Sorrow for company, felt like a great relief. It was as if, for the first time she could recall, no one was watching her.

And what would Ama do with this first secret freedom?

She pulled Sorrow up from where she lay in the crook of Ama's knees, wrapped her arms around the lynx's warm, soft pelt, and sobbed into her neck, the kit lapping up her tears with her rough tongue.

Ama wept. Until, at last, she slept.

Ama did not hear the turn of the knob. She did not hear the creak of the door, pushed open. She did not hear the footsteps cross the floorboards of her room.

But when the bed curtain was pulled back, with a whisper of cloth just near her head—that, Ama did hear.

She woke, breath trapped in her throat, a sick roll of her stomach, room spinning in the dark—from fear or wine, Ama did not know. At her side, still clutched in her arms, Sorrow growled, a low and dreadful sound.

"Call off your guard, Ama," came Emory's voice. "It is I."

Ama stroked Sorrow's pelt, and though some part of her felt that perhaps Sorrow's warning was not unwarranted, she hushed the cat until the growling stopped.

"Make room for me," Emory said, and Ama shifted over in her bed so that Emory could sit down beside her.

She raised herself up onto her elbows, and would have sat fully erect but for Emory's insistent hand on her shoulder, pinning her there, and then his insistent mouth slashing down across her own.

His mouth was hot and wet and open and tasted of the evening's wine and meat. Underneath the weight of him—his mouth, first, and then his chest across hers, pressing Ama back into the mattress—Ama felt breathless and trapped, as if she had been submerged underwater.

This had felt like her own room earlier in the evening, but now it was clear that the room, and everything it contained—including Ama herself—was the property of the castle, and of Emory, as master of it.

Only her one hand, which rested still on Sorrow's back, felt like Ama's own. The rest of her became part of the landscape of the room—her lips, pressed into Emory's teeth. Her hair, torn from its neat plait by his desperate hand. Her breast, when he shifted his weight up and slipped his hand down from her head to her chest, pulling apart the ribbons of her chemise, spreading open the cloth, and finding her bare skin beneath. His hand squeezed her flesh as if he would try to make something from it, and the calluses of his palm rubbed across her nipple, causing it to harden, which Ama noticed as if watching from some distance rather than from within the very skin he handled.

But when Emory tugged up at the hem of Ama's shift, bunching its fabric at her waist and running his hand first across the downy nest of hair between her legs and then pushing his fingers inside of her, opening her in a way she had not known she could be opened, Sorrow growled once more.

This time, Ama loosened her fingers from the lynx's pelt, a silent permission to do what Ama could not.

Wild now, the lynx arched her back and hissed, eyes glowing in the last of the fire. Her claws were black talons, and she stretched them menacingly. Lips pulled back from her fangs, Sorrow was dangerous and feral.

Emory's hand froze, fingers knuckle-deep in Ama, and then, slowly, he withdrew it, leaving her bruised and undone.

Emory cleared his throat, lifted himself from the bed, and arranged his yard, which stood in his trousers, hard and demanding.

"Forgive me," he said, to Ama or to Sorrow, she did not know. "I am addled by the wine and your presence here, in my castle. There will be time, after solstice, for such things."

And he bowed, and he dropped the bed curtain, and he turned for the door.

But before he left the room, he said one more thing: "By our wedding night, Ama, that creature will be gone."

Tillie's Aunt

When Ama awoke again, it was to the sounds of the ladies in her room. The fire was built back up, the bed curtains pulled open.

Tillie was there, and Ama was glad to see her freckled face. It was Tillie who offered Ama the chamber pot, though it was Rohesia who took it away after.

A girl who had helped serve at dinner the night before brought Ama a tray from the kitchen. Her face, unlike Tillie's, was not open to Ama; eyes downcast, surly-mouthed, she delivered the tray to Ama's bed with apathetic duty. When she put it in Ama's lap, the hot morning drink splashed out of its cup.

"Take care, Fabiana!" Tillie reprimanded.

"My apologies," Fabiana said, with a quick curtsy that Ama could tell was clearly perfunctory.

"That girl," Tillie said, mopping up the spilled beverage. "Don't pay her any mind."

"She seems unhappy," Ama said.

Tillie looked as if she might say more, but instead she pushed the tray to Ama and said, "Eat while you can, lady. We have a day in front of us, we do."

And so they did. Much of the morning was spent pulling on and taking off various gowns for the coronation, while Tillie took measurements and Rohesia took notes. There were a half dozen of them, plus underdressings, and a cloak and cape, as well.

Ama gave herself over to Tillie's practiced hands, and she thought, as Tillie fastened up the final gown, that she much preferred having her body touched like this, in a detached and utilitarian manner, to the way Emory had touched it the night before.

She obligingly held up her arms as Tillie checked the gown's fit, turned this way and that as Tillie measured the hem.

"Do you prefer this gown or the last?" Tillie asked.

"The last," Ama said. "It was looser in the chest. I could breathe more easily."

"That is not what I meant," Tillie said. "Which gown did you prefer the look of? Which do you think was more becoming?"

"Oh," said Ama. "I have no preference about that. Whichever you think, I am sure."

Tillie smiled. "My aunt told me that the queen mother had no preferences of this sort either, when she first came to the castle. But she learned, she did, and now she is well known for her sharp eye about what flatters her best. You will be the same, I wager, in time."

This caught Ama's attention. What was it that the queen mother had said last night, at dinner? That Emory had rescued a damsel from a dragon, and "earned his position as tradition dictates." That meant that the queen mother herself must have once been a damsel as well. "Tillie," Ama said, "tell me more about the queen mother."

"Well, she wasn't born here, of course. She was like you—saved from a dragon, rescued by the king." Tillie's tongue was loosened by her attention to her work, bending to measure, calling out to Rohesia, standing, turning Ama, measuring again. "All kings, for as far back as our memory goes, are made the same way. The prince must venture alone away from Harding. He must find a dragon. He must conquer the dragon and free the damsel from captivity. When he returns home with his prize, he has proven himself worthy of the crown and is made king."

"Tell me," Ama said, wanting to hear the answer from Tillie, "did the queen mother have any people—people who knew her before she was taken by the dragon, who came to Harding to celebrate her rescue and her marriage to the king?"

Tillie stopped her work, straightened, frowned. "Oh, no," she said. "The damsel never has people, you know, until she is a wife and then a mother. And it's her very son whose coronation is almost upon us, my lady. It's just hours before you will be presented to the court and crowd as his queen-in-waiting. That is why

I wonder—this gown, or the other?"

"This gown will do," Ama said, gazing at her reflection in the long ovular mirror. The queen mother had no people. And Ama had no people, just the same.

"It is funny you pick this gown," Tillie said, "for it is the very gown the queen mother chose twenty years ago, when she was presented to court and crowd as the queen-in-waiting."

"Oh?" said Ama. "How do you know that? Surely that was well before your time."

"My aunt helped me unpack these gowns from storage, in anticipation of your arrival," Tillie said. "She served the queen mother in her first months here at the castle, just as I serve you."

Ama regarded the wide velvet swoop of the gown's purple arms. She saw reflected her own hands, turned to reverse in the mirror glass. "I would like to meet this aunt of yours," she said to Tillie. "Bring her to me, please."

It was, Ama thought, as Tillie bowed her head and left to fetch her aunt, the first order Ama had given.

Tillie's aunt came to Ama's room, her face obscured by a veil. "You called for me, lady?" she said, dropping a deep curtsy. Her gown was not the rough-hewn hemp of the lesser servants, but a flat black of sturdy material. It was plain by design, her dress, severely plain.

"I did," said Ama. "Tillie tells me that you served the queen mother when she first came to the castle. I hope you might be able to help me learn my place here, as you have seen a damsel arrive to the castle before."

"It is not for me to tell a queen-in-waiting her place," Tillie's aunt said. "If anything, it is for her to tell me mine."

"Your place," said Ama, "right now, is here, at my ear. And I implore you to speak freely, and tell me what you can of the queen mother and the other damsels who have come before me."

Tillie's aunt said nothing. Ama felt as though she was being studied, very closely, through the veil that shrouded the woman's face.

For a moment, she gave herself over to being examined, but she found she was tired of being the object of others' gazes. "What is your name?" she asked Tillie's aunt.

"Allys, it is," Tillie's aunt replied.

"Allys," said Ama. "Please, remove your veil. If you shall regard me with such a look, then I wish to see your face just as clearly."

Allys bowed her head and brought her hands to her veil. She took it up at its hem and folded it back across her head of steel-gray hair.

And then she raised her gaze, and Ama looked into her face—and into her one green eye.

Allys's Advice

Where the other eye should have been, there was instead just darkness. A half-closed lid, sunken in, and nothing more.

Ama felt her mouth fall open, and forced herself to close it, to turn her gaze from the missing eye to Allys's remaining eye, green and perceptive, watching now as Ama stared.

"Does it disgust you, lady?" Allys asked.

"No," Ama said, and her voice was steady. "It makes me wonder."

"Yes," said Allys, "that it does." But she did not offer an answer to Ama's unasked question. Instead she said, "What can I tell you, lady?"

"Please," said Ama, "tell me about the queen mother's early days, when she was a damsel new to this place."

"She was a beauty," Allys began, as if this was unquestionably the most important piece of information she could offer. "Ink-black hair, and shiny, it was. Eyes of amber. A figure worth rescuing, no matter the risk. Bosoms, tremendous bosoms, a waist no bigger around than the king's hands could hold. Small feet. Pretty hands."

Her eye ran up and down Ama's body as she spoke, and there was a tone to her voice that told a different story than the words she said aloud—her tone and her roaming gaze clearly said that the queen mother had been more beautiful than Ama, shapelier, more feminine, finer. Next to the queen mother when she arrived, Ama would have been but a shadow, if that.

But Ama did not mind. She found herself not terribly attached to her body or what others might think of it.

"What of her mind?" Ama asked. "What did she remember?"

"Remember?" Allys asked.

"Yes," said Ama. "Remember. Of the time before her rescue. Of her life, before."

Allys smiled, and her green eye twinkled. "Nothing, of course," she said. "The damsels have no memory."

"Never?" said Ama.

"Never," said Allys, as if she dared Ama to tell her she was wrong.

"But . . . why?"

"I have learned, lady, that 'why' is a dangerous word."

Tillie, who had stood quietly by, looking vaguely uncomfortable by the conversation's path, stepped in to say, "If that is all, lady, we really must return to our preparations for the coronation. You will be expected to be elegant and well-coiffed."

"This is an important day for you," Allys agreed. "The court and crowds will take their first measure of you, and you mustn't come up short." She bowed and turned to take her leave.

"But you have told me nothing," Ama said, and she was angry.

Allys turned back around. "There is nothing to tell you," Allys answered. "The damsels are a legacy of nothing—no memory, no past, no family. Accept your nothing, and pray it stays that way."

"Pray it stays that way, you say?"

Allys's eye darted around the room.

"So you say there *is* something for me to remember," Ama pressed.

Allys grimaced. She said nothing.

Ama waited.

At last Allys said, "Lady, you are the third damsel I have seen in this castle. I have seen one damsel who moved forward, and one damsel who spun back. I have seen great joy, and I have seen terrible heartbreak. I have seen power, and I have seen weakness. You ask me what I can tell you. And I can tell you this: The castle is your home. King Emory will be your husband. There is only forward."

Ama looked into Allys's one eye. She did not know what she searched for, there.

"Please," she said to Allys, "tell me something, then, of the king."

"Something of the king," Allys repeated.

"Is Emory a good man?" Ama asked. She felt desperate now. Her dress was too tight. Her feet were cold. The place between her legs was tender, and her eyes filled with tears.

Allys did not answer straightaway. Instead, she looked at Sorrow, who had finished her morning meal and was batting about a length of fabric that Tillie had cut from the hem of one of Ama's gowns.

"Tell me," she said to Ama, "which makes a more pleasing pet—a cat or a rabbit?"

"A cat," said Ama at once.

"Yes," said Allys. "A cat. And do you know why?"

Ama considered. "Because they are more playful?"

"Perhaps," Allys answered. "Or, perhaps, because they are more dangerous."

Sorrow pounced on the fabric strip, pinned it between her front paws, and tore it in two with her teeth.

"Don't be a rabbit, lady," said Allys. "Everyone with a head about them prefers a cat. I should know," she added wryly, "being but a rabbit, myself."

Ama pressed on. "I have a third question—and the last, I promise."

"About my eye, is it?"

Ama nodded. "Tell me," she said, "what did you wish for when you took an Eye from the wall? What need had you, so great as to risk an eye?"

Allys blinked her one remaining eye. "It is not a nice story, lady," she said.

"Yes," said Ama. "That much I guessed."

Tillie said, as if she wished to spare her aunt from having to tell the tale, "Years ago, before I was born, when she was in service to the queen, my aunt drew the . . . attention of a man here at the castle. It was unwanted, and often violent."

Ama turned to Allys. "Violent?"

"The tastes of men are not all kind," Allys said. "I was the unfortunate recipient of this man's unfortunate predilections."

Ama asked, "Who was this man?"

"It does not matter," Allys answered. "Only to say that I had no power, and I feared for my life."

"So you went to the wall," Ama said, "and you took an Eye, and you wished for this man to die?"

Allys barked a laugh. "That may have been a wiser wish than the one I cast," she said. And then, "But I told you, lady, I am a rabbit, not a cat. I did not wish for his death. I wished only for my safety. To be left alone by him, that is all I asked when I went to the wall and plucked out an Eye. It was a green one, I remember, the brightest green." She paused for a moment, as if picturing the stolen Eye in her hand. Then she turned to Ama and fixed her in her singular gaze. "They caught me with the Eye almost as soon as I had managed to pry it from its mortar. There was no need for a trial. No one had ever been more plainly guilty than I was, and so they took the wall's Eye from my hand, and one of mine from my head, and sent me on my way."

"Oh," said Ama. "But you were only trying to protect yourself!"

"Law is law," Allys answered. "I swooned from the pain, and my sister—this one's mother—brought me home. I caught fever from infection and near died, I did. It was weeks before I healed, and weeks more before I could work again. But I lived. I lived. And when I was in my own head again, I found that the man I so feared wanted no more to do with me, disfigured as I was.

"So you see, lady, my wish was granted, after all."

FOUR

Emory's Coronation

Tillie had found a leather collar for Sorrow, and though Ama hated the idea of restraining the lynx, she hated even more the thought of leaving her behind. When she first fastened the collar around Sorrow's neck, the lynx kitten flopped onto her side and clawed at it with her back paws.

It was on tightly enough not to come off over her head with such treatment, but not so tightly as to cause discomfort, and when Ama offered her a piece of smoked fish as distraction, Sorrow accepted it, and the collar, as well.

The leash was made of fine gold chain, cool and slippery in Ama's hand, with a leather strap for a handle. Tillie connected leash to collar and handed it to Ama, who practiced for some minutes leading the kit about the room.

Sorrow was a smart student, and though it was certain that she would have preferred freedom to being chained, regular rewards of smoked fish and scratches behind her ears seemed to convince her to be complacent enough.

And she was still small enough that Ama could carry her if Sorrow grew overwhelmed by the crowds, though if she grew as big as her mother had been, this would not always be an option.

And Emory said Sorrow must be gone before the wedding night, Ama thought.

Sorrow would not be yet full-grown by midwinter. She would be a gangly youth, at best. What would her chances be, alone in the forest, and in the cold?

So Ama had a goal: She must convince Emory to allow her to keep Sorrow past the wedding, at least, and, perhaps, for always.

"The coronation will take place out of doors, on the high balcony," Tillie said, picking up a fur-trimmed mantle from a chair. "Your lynx will be warm enough, but you should wear this." She swung the mantle across Ama's shoulders and fastened it at her left shoulder with a large broach.

Ama liked the weight of the cloak; she liked the gilded blue-stoned clasp; she liked the soft fluff of dark fur against her cheek, with the hood pulled up over her hair.

"You cut a fine figure, you do," Tillie said. "The king should be well pleased to have you at his side."

Ama took up the leather strap of Sorrow's golden leash. The lynx, smart as she was, followed close as Ama crossed the room to the mirror. There was a lady there, amber eyes shaded by the fur-trimmed hood, a lady with a ribbon-laced red braid across her breast, a purple velvet gown, and a lynx, sharp of tooth and claw, at her heel.

The lady in the mirror looked like someone Ama would be pleased to know and like a complete stranger, both at the same time.

"You are ready." Tillie sounded certain, and Ama, a stranger to her very own skin, felt it smarter to rely on what Tillie knew than what she herself might feel.

Tillie said she was ready; and so Ama went.

Just inside the high balcony, Ama found Emory waiting for her.

"And when I thought you couldn't be lovelier," he said, with a sweeping bow, "here you come, a delight of velvet and fur, to prove me wrong. Your lynx companion makes for a lovely accessory, I shall grant you that."

Emory reached out for Ama's hand, and she hesitated only a second before extending it. He flipped her hand over and kissed her there, in the soft white center of her palm.

Then he pulled her close and whispered into her ear, "Dearest, please accept my apology for my appearance last night in your quarters. It is certainly not my character to act in . . . such a passion-fueled manner. But who could blame me, when a beauty such as yourself is under my roof, and so close to being my wife? Certainly, many men would not have been able to restrain themselves at all, confronted with the same situation."

He withdrew slightly, so that Ama could see into his deep-blue eyes, so that Ama could see his softly tilting smile.

She felt her own mouth pull into a returning smile, and cast her gaze down. "I thank you for your uncommon restraint, my lord," she answered.

"The time will come soon enough that such restraint shall not be required of me," Emory said. "And that is a day I truly look toward. Until then, I shall try not to allow your feminine powers to induce me to another such visit."

Ama dropped a curtsy, as best she could with her one hand still taken up by Emory's and her other hand clutching Sorrow's leash.

She was relieved when she heard the rustling of the queen mother's skirts behind her and Emory released her hand to greet her.

"Mother," he said, voice full and loud now, "you look positively charming."

Ama turned and curtsied.

The queen mother's gown, built of a sharp black taffeta, was covered all over by a flowering bloom of gems—on her chest, a bouquet designed of rubies, citrines, sapphires, and diamonds; and down her waist and across the vast expanse of her skirt wound curlicues of thorn-laced stems, rendered in ropes of emeralds. She did not wear a cape, most probably because she did not want to obscure the fine jewel work of her gown, but her hair was up in a vine-like network of braids, with roses of pink gems tucked into the filigree of the rose-gold crown that circled her head.

"Ama," she said, when Ama rose from her curtsy, "you must introduce me to this glorious pet of yours."

"Certainly, Queen Mother," Ama said, hoping desperately that the lynx would receive her silent pleas to behave herself. "This is the kit I call Sorrow."

The queen mother offered her hand, and Sorrow sniffed it, then extended her pretty pink tongue in a kiss.

"A darling," the queen mother said admiringly, and scratched the cat between the ears. Sorrow stepped forward and rubbed her head against the queen mother's skirt and purred, a deep rumble of a sound.

The queen mother laughed, delighted. "I believe your Sorrow finds in me a sympathetic friend," she said, and then looked up at Ama with an expression so searing that Ama felt laid bare by it, as if the force of the gaze had burned her clothes from her limbs, and her skin, as well.

"I hope Sorrow's mistress finds me equally sympathetic," she said.

"Indeed," Ama answered at once, for she knew it was the correct answer, whether it was the truth or not.

"You must visit me in my chambers and meet my pets," the queen mother continued.

Ama bowed her head in thanks for the invitation.

"Shall we?" Emory said, and then they turned—Emory at the center, flanked by the queen mother on his right and Ama, herself accompanied by Sorrow, on his left.

Guards opened the doors to the high balcony, and Ama was assaulted by a rush of sound and cold. They stepped onto the stone, into an icy wetness—not quite rain, not quite sleet—and the rumble of the crowd mounted into a deafening roar. Emory and the queen mother raised their hands in greeting, and Ama did, as well. At her side, Sorrow mewled and pressed against her, overwhelmed by the crowd.

Ama felt overwhelmed too, looking down upon the throng of people below—how long had they stood in this weather, waiting for a glimpse of their king?—and bent to scoop the lynx into her arms. She tucked her beneath her cloak and pulled it closed, protecting her from the roar of the crowd.

There were red-faced children down there, snot streaming from their noses, some with no shoes. There were women suckling babes and men waving small banners, the Harding insignia, Ama guessed, painted onto them: a green dragon, and behind it, the shadow figure of a king.

The banners were everywhere—on handheld flags, on waving banners, on tapestries that hung on either side of the high balcony.

Ama had the prickly sensation of having walked into someone else's story—a story in which everyone but she knew their role and their lines. The king's job was to conquer. Emory had proved admirable at that, no one could say otherwise. The dragon's job was to be vanquished, and, as there was currently no dragon to be seen other than the rough illustrations all around, it seemed the dragon had done its job, as well.

But between the dragon and the king, there should have been a third figure, Ama thought. There should have been a damsel.

"Smile," Emory hissed into her ear, his own face curled into a grin, "and wave. The people are waiting for you."

Ama arranged her face as she was told. She grasped the lynx close and raised her hand to the people below. They exploded into cheers, and beneath her cloak, hidden from everyone, Sorrow dug her claws into Ama's chest, dampening the fine velvet gown with blood.

The Musicians' Song

The great hall had undergone a near-magical transformation from when last Ama had seen it, late the night before. Then it had been almost empty, and shadowy, and solemn, as well. Now, when Ama entered it at the coronation's finish, on the arm of her king, it was the site of a raucous, jubilant celebration.

Elegantly dressed bodies crammed shoulder against shoulder, waiting to congratulate King Emory and meet his damsel prize. Some of the people wore tall, elaborate wigs; some were roped with jewels; some looked squeezed into their coats and dresses, as if the meal they were about to eat would burst the already-strained seams; others looked as though their natural state was in this elegant dress, carrying themselves almost as if they floated.

A trio of musicians plucked at their stringed instruments, but the sound they produced was barely audible, overlaid by the voices of the crowd—loud chatter, piercing laughter, here and there an argument, heated tones of conflict waxing and then waning like the moon.

Ama was glad she had sent Sorrow back to her room with Tillie; this was no place for a nervous animal. She wished she could have excused herself from the feast as well. But Emory had a firm grip on her hand, raised high, and he seemed as intent to show her off as he was the new crown he wore on his head—a heavy ring of three interwoven metals, platinum, bronze, and rose gold, which crested in a series of dangerous-looking spikes all around.

Unlike the queen mother's crown, which had been soft in its lines, though clearly of great worth, Emory's new headpiece looked as deadly as a weapon, each spike a sharp-tipped point, the three metals of which it was built locked in a battle for dominance.

All of the people wanted to touch Ama and Emory. Hand after hand extended to her as Emory introduced her to an endless stream of his closest friends and advisers.

"This is the Duke and Duchess of Cromming," Emory told Ama, and the duke kissed her hand, then the duchess held it by the fingers as she curtsied.

"This is Father Jacob," Emory next said as the round-faced priest bobbed his head at Ama's hand, clutched in his sweaty grasp.

On and on it went, the introductions, and with each curtsy, each kiss, each grasp of her hand, Ama felt as if she were the mutton on the table, being consumed bite after bite.

They were seated at last, and only when everyone was at the tables did the queen mother enter, avoiding the crush of greeters and slipping smoothly into her seat beside the king.

She saw Ama's envious expression and laughed. "I had my years of receiving," she said. "It is your turn now, to bear that burden."

And then the meal began, and the crowd hushed over their meat and mead, so Ama could hear the musicians' song clearly at last.

She realized at once that never before had she heard anything like this—like *music*. Not in the time since Emory rescued her from the dragon, and, she knew with absolute clarity of mind, not before that, either.

It was the closest she had to a memory: this surety of absence, this knowledge that never before had her ears heard a song. It was a truth that belonged only to her, a secret that she tucked away like a hidden jewel.

There was meat on her plate and mead in her cup, but Ama wanted neither. She tilted her head toward the musicians, closed her eyes to better concentrate on the tune, and breathed as quietly as she could.

It was a song of joy and celebration; that was clear. Quick, loud, upbeat. Two of the musicians plucked the notes from the strings, but the third drew a bow across his instrument to release his song. Together, the three instruments braided separate notes into something greater than any of them could produce alone. Ama's heart felt both full and light in the same moment.

"Are you all right?" Emory asked, breaking her focus.

Ama's eyes snapped open. She was back in the opulent, overcrowded hall, stuffed with bodies and smells—so many smells, the meat and the vegetables, oily in butter and juices; the mead, sour and heavy; the bodies around her; and her own flesh, as well, constricted in the too-tight velvet, stewing as if she were another dish.

"I am fine," she answered. "I was just listening to the music."

"Well, eat your meat," Emory demanded, pointing with his knife down the long table. "Everyone else has stopped feasting in deference to you."

It was true, Ama saw. All up and down the table, forks and knives were suspended midair, or laid aside, as the court watched her face and waited for her to enjoy her meal.

The terrible burden of everyone's eyes upon her face made any hunger Ama may have felt disappear completely.

Still, this was her duty, one of many, Ama was learning, and so she smiled and took up a forkful of potato, brought it to her mouth. Chewed. Swallowed.

The table guests, satisfied, returned to their own plates, and after a moment of eating slowly, Ama saw that there was some shelter in doing as she was expected to do; it was when she broke from her role that attention felt especially heavy.

When she busied herself with raising and lowering her fork, and then her cup, and then her napkin, she seemed to fade into the texture of the room. At her side, leaning back in his chair to survey the hall, Emory emitted a palpable air of satisfaction.

"It's lovely, isn't it, Ama?" he asked, gesturing expansively—at the golden platters overflowing with food, the pitchers full of drink, the musicians in their corner, the rainbow of satins and silks all down the long table. "It's my one sadness that Pawlin was not home from his hunt in time for the coronation. He does love a good feast."

"I am sure he will be glad to hear the news when he returns, my king."

"Undoubtedly," Emory said, and his gaze landed softly on Ama. "And better still will be to share with him that I have found my damsel." Emory's hand, a warm weight, settled on Ama's. "All of this is sweeter, my love, with you at my side."

Ama's fingers spread to allow Emory's to interlace. It was a comfort, in a way, the weight and presence of his hand.

"Such a lovely couple." It was the prior who had spoken the ceremonial words at Emory's coronation, a man spiderlike in the length of his limbs, his white hair a web atop his head. He had shed his formal crimson robes from the rite and was dressed now in a rich, black cassock that fell in a straight line from chin to toes.

He had not, Ama noticed, set aside his jewelry; the sharp-tipped triangular pendant still hung on its polished silver chain around his neck, and an assortment of seven rings still bejeweled the four fingers of his right hand and all but the pointer finger of his left.

As he spoke with Emory about the coronation—the size of the crowd, the good fortune of heavy rain staying away from the day—Ama found she could not look away from the rings. On the prior's left hand were a yellow stone, a green stone, and a purple stone; on the right were a blue stone, a red stone, an indigo stone, and an orange stone.

"Have you considered wearing the purple stone on the right hand, and the blue stone on the left?" Ama blurted at last, when she could stand it no longer.

Emory's lip curled slightly, as if he had smelled something unfortunate.

"What is that, girl?" asked the prior, leaning in to hear.

She had interrupted him midsentence, Ama realized now, and her face flushed with shame.

"Forgive me," she said, and cast down her eyes.

The men turned back toward each other to continue their conversation.

"It's only," Ama said, her voice louder than she intended, "you see, if you were to trade the blue-stoned ring for the purple—and you could, couldn't you, each is on a middle finger—if you were to switch them, Prior, then the colors of the stones on your right hand could all be made by combining the colors from the stones on your left hand."

"She is new to our ways, Prior," said the king, smoothly interjecting. "You must forgive her impertinence."

"I shall do better than that," said the prior with a quick smile. "I shall humor it." And he slipped off the blue ring and the purple, rearranging them in the way Ama had suggested. "Better?" he asked.

"Much," Ama answered, and she bobbed her head in thanks. "Don't they please the eye this way?"

Now, Ama noticed, quite a crowd of people was listening to their conversation and watching as the prior regarded his hands.

"'Tis not for my station to pay heed to such things," said the prior at last, "but, yes, your highness, I suppose they do please the eye this way, as well as the other."

Emory cleared his throat. "I must thank you, Prior, for your fine speech at the coronation."

"Oh, my king," the prior said, swishing his skirt as he bowed, "what a pleasure it was to officiate. It is not every prior who has the great honor of coronating two kings. You cut a figure in that crown that nearly twinned that of your father, only taller. You know," he said, turning to Ama, "I will also have the pleasure of wedding two queens to their kings."

"Is that so?" Ama said.

"Indeed, it is," the prior said. He turned to Emory with a wink. "But the bedding, my king, is entirely your duty."

The two men laughed, and Ama felt herself blush, wished she could turn herself inside out, or disappear. She felt a jolt of shame, for what she did not know. She longed to be anywhere, anywhere but here, and her eyes cast about the table as if for escape.

There, in the table's center, was a fat-bottomed violet glass bowl, half full of water, in which several candles floated, their tiny flames steady and bright, reflecting up from the water and off the sides of the bowl. It was lovely to Ama. This must be one of the glassblower's creations, she thought, and thinking of the glassblower turned her mind to the Eyes in the wall, Eyes that watched and Eyes that judged, Eyes that perhaps granted wishes, if one dared to ask. It was loud and crowded in the great hall, too loud and too crowded, by far, but Ama sat very still and let her own eyes blur as she watched the flicker of light on water and glass.

Isolda's Jesses

The next morning was still cold, colder, perhaps, than the day before, but the sky outside of Ama's window was a clear bright blue. In the sky hung a cold, distant sun, flat and painful to look at, though Ama's eyes returned to it again and again, as if drawn there by some magnetism.

Her heart hurt, a dull ache, when she gazed at the sun, and there was a sharp pain behind her eyes, as well. But she found it difficult to look away. A word came to her—"homesick"—and Ama blinked, rubbed her eyes, turned back to her room and her fire.

Now, as if the sun had been printed on her eyes, everywhere she looked Ama saw its shadow, small black circles floating in her field of vision. She played with this effect, closing one eye and then the other, regarding her room, her fire, and her lynx through the specter of ghost suns that she alone could see, until they faded, and faded, and disappeared, and her room was ordinary once more.

Nothing, though, was ordinary about her lynx. Ama regarded her with a mother's pride, the way she stretched long in front of the fire, her tawny coat, her black-tipped ears, her oversize paws front and back, her funny bobbed tail.

"You have been indoors too long, I think," Ama told the kit. "We both have."

So, when Tillie returned to the room for another session of gown fitting, this time for the wedding dress that would take weeks to create, Ama said to her, "We shall do that another time. Now, I require my cloak and Sorrow's leash. She and I are going out of doors."

Tillie bowed her head and did as she was asked, helping Ama step into leather overshoes and covering Ama's shoulders with the fur-trimmed cloak. Ama fastened its broach, pulled on the gloves Tillie gave to her, and took up Sorrow's leash.

"Would you like company, lady?" Tillie asked.

"I am never alone when I have my Sorrow," Ama answered. "Perhaps you could take some time for yourself while I am out of doors."

Tillie regarded her blankly, unblinking in a way that made Ama blush. It was untoward of her to suggest such a thing, she saw at once. But nevertheless, she forged ahead. "You are welcome to stay here, if you would like, and enjoy the fire and breakfast tray."

Then, before Tillie could answer, Ama turned for the door, Sorrow's claws clicking on the hard floor beside her.

But once on the staircase, Ama allowed fear to seep in. She had no idea where she was going or how she could find her way back to her own room.

"Never mind all that," she told Sorrow, though Sorrow did not look as if she had been fretting. "We shall figure that out later. For now, let us find the gardens."

It was several staircases and many misturns later that Ama found a door that led her outside. She had ignored the curious looks from the servants she encountered and found herself hoping that she would not run into Emory on her way out of the castle.

Perhaps he would not let her go outside, Ama thought, which made her feel queasy.

But stepping across the threshold into the outside world blew all such thoughts straight from her mind. Ama felt herself smiling as she stretched her arms wide, standing on an expansive black stone porch, wrapped around with pillars of the same ebony stone, and filled her chest with cold, clean air.

Sorrow nipped at her skirt hem, urging her back into motion, and Ama started off again briskly, hopping down the stairs to the hard, flat ground. "Let's see where this path takes us, shall we?" she said to her lynx companion, and it was clear by the trot Sorrow took up that she was well pleased with this adventure.

Ama's attention was divided by the blue of the sky, the white of the sun disc in it, the satisfying crunch of the dirt and pebbles beneath her leather shoes, the frigid breath of the cold fall air on her face, the exquisitely soft brush of her hood's fur against her cheek, the joyful gait of the lynx at her side.

All is well, she thought suddenly, and she felt happy. She wandered, the black castle at her back, the weight of it feeling lighter and lighter the farther from it she stepped.

And then she rounded a tall bend in the hedges and found herself in an enclosed space—ten-foot hedges all around, bigger than her personal chamber but smaller than the great hall, open but for a smaller, round planter of hedges at its center, these trimmed to waist height. All of the hedges here, like elsewhere on the castle grounds, were dormant for the winter months, leaves gone, a network of branches that would grow anew with spring's arrival. By the time the leaves had sprouted and flowers had bloomed, Ama would be a wife, and a queen.

She dismissed this thought and knelt down at Sorrow's side. The kitten was sniffing around in the dirt, and paused to look into Ama's eyes. Ama felt her own eyes burn with tears, as if she had been struck, as if to be looked at by the kit, with such clarity, was painful.

"This is surely a safe place to let you romp," Ama said, and she loosed the collar from Sorrow's neck and dropped it and the leash to the ground.

Pleased, Sorrow trotted around the space, and Ama followed her. The kitten squatted to relieve herself, her puddle of urine spreading across the dry dirt.

"Ho, what's this?"

It was a man's voice, suddenly, from the split in the hedge through which Ama had entered.

She turned around, instinctively grabbing closed the neck of her mantle.

"I've surprised you," said the man with a grin.

It was a nice enough grin, on a handsome enough man, but neither the grin nor the man caught Ama's attention nearly as much as the bird he carried.

It was a great black hawk, with rust-colored feathers on her wings and legs, and scaly yellow claws that ended in vicious talons. She stared at Ama with unblinking brown eyes. From her eyes to her black beak, her face was the same yellow as her feet. Her hooked beak ended in a dangerous spike. Her expression was either haughty or desperately sad—Ama could not tell which.

"You are Pawlin," Ama said, "and this is Isolda, I presume?"

"Correct on both counts," Pawlin said with a bow, a mocking sweep of his short cloak. He kept his hawk arm parallel with the ground as he bowed, clearly well-practiced. "And you are the lady Ama," Pawlin said, his grin widening.

"That is what I have been told," Ama answered.

"Clever as well as lovely," Pawlin said, and whether it was a compliment or an assessment made no difference.

Sorrow, who had finished relieving her bladder, returned to

Ama's side on careful paws, her eyes trained on the hawk.

"Your beast is a beauty," Pawlin remarked, and his appreciation was clear now. "Tell me about her."

Ama knelt and scooped up the kit, who was already heavier since their arrival to the castle. "This is my Sorrow," she said.

"An unfortunate name for a pet," Pawlin said. "Perhaps you should consider something more . . . sporting. Bounder, for instance. Or Fleetfoot."

Those were, Ama felt, perfectly terrible names. "Thank you for your ideas," she demurred, "but Sorrow is her name, and so it shall remain."

Pawlin narrowed his eyes, and Ama had the impression that he, like Emory, was not a man who often heard his ideas rebuffed.

But he was not Emory, and she had no liege with him, so she lifted her chin and dared him to say another thing about it.

"I do wonder," Pawlin said, "who would take the prize in a contest between your beast and mine." He stroked the sleek feathers on Isolda's back and, Ama would swear, Isolda smiled, though a beak cannot smile.

"My Sorrow is not yet grown," Ama said. "When she is, I am certain she would be the victor."

"But today," Pawlin said, and his free hand went to the jesses on his gauntlet, "I wonder about today."

Ama watched with growing horror as Pawlin's fingers took up the thin, knotted leather strips and began to pull.

Sorrow's Leash

Ama clutched the lynx kitten close to her chest as Pawlin's fingers freed the first set of leather straps. Now the hawk's left foot was unfettered. She watched as he slowly moved toward the second set of jesses, as he prepared to pull them apart, his eyes locked on her face, his mouth grinning terribly.

"Please," gasped Ama, uttering the word that had worked such power with Emory, "I beg you, please. My Sorrow is all I have, all that is mine."

"*All* that you have?" Pawlin said, his fingers pausing midair. "What of your king?"

"Of course," Ama said, all in a rush, "I have him, as well. I have Emory."

"I wonder if you do," Pawlin said, and he was not smiling now. "Indeed, I wonder if *he* truly has *you*."

Ama had no idea what he could mean by this. Of *course* Emory had her—he had freed her from the dragon, he had brought her here to the castle, he had trapped her in his walls and this velvet gown and these leather shoes. She was his, sure as the sun.

"Indeed, he has," Ama breathed, and she hated how weak her voice sounded, how much power Pawlin had, right now, in the very tips of his fingers. For if he were to pull free that last knot, then Isolda would attack, there was no doubt of that. She was a hunter, with claws and beak to catch and tear.

Would he have loosed the knot? Would she have held her own Sorrow in her arms as the great hawk tore open her throat, as Emory's weapon had torn open her mother's?

She was not to know, not today, for at that moment, there was a rustle once more from the divide in the hedges, and Emory appeared.

Never had Ama been so grateful to see him. A little sound like a cry slipped from her lips, and, the kitten still clutched in her arms, she ran to him.

"My king," she said, and his arms wound around her waist, her head tucked under his chin. Between their bodies, safe now, protected, was Sorrow.

"What's this?" boomed Emory. "My friend and my lady, in a secret meeting in this winter's garden?" Perhaps he was jesting. Perhaps he was not. It was not possible to tell.

"I wanted to get out of doors," Ama said, hating the sound of her own voice. "And the air was so fresh, and the day so fine, that I walked for a long time and found myself here."

"I wonder that you did not send word for my company, or at least my consent," Emory said. "What a disappointment."

Ama pulled away from the crook of Emory's neck, into which she had buried her face, and tilted her eyes to Emory's. But he was not looking at her; he was looking at Pawlin. Ama did the same, turning to regard Pawlin, who had refastened Isolda's jesses. His face and the bird's were twin masks of haughty unknowableness.

"Pawlin," Emory said, his voice friendly now. "I did not know you had returned from the hunt."

"I arrived with the sun this morning," Pawlin said, smiling. "I would have hurried on the road home had I known you would be so quick with your own expedition, my lord."

"'Tis 'my king,' now, isn't it?" said Emory, gesturing to his crown.

"As I heard, my king," Pawlin answered, and though he said the right words and made the right bows, his tone and carriage did not denote the difference in their ranks.

This did not seem to bother Emory, who laughed loud and walked away from Ama to clasp Pawlin by his shoulders in a rough embrace.

"So, it has come to pass," Pawlin said when they split apart, "and your damsel prize is every bit as lovely as the legends told she would be."

"Lovelier," Emory said, an edge to his voice.

"Lovelier," Pawlin corrected. "Indeed, lovelier."

Now they were both appraising her, and Isolda too, and had she not held Sorrow in her arms, she would have felt naked under the scrutiny of their shared gaze.

"Lovely," Emory said, "yes. But obedient . . . perhaps, no. Not yet."

"Please, my king," Ama begged, but for what, she knew not.

Emory bent and retrieved Sorrow's leash from where Ama had laid it aside. He wrapped the golden chain around his fist—once, twice, three times—and walked slowly to Ama's side.

"Dearest Ama," he said, and his voice was gentle. It was playful. Was it not?

Sorrow growled low but fierce, and Ama dug her fingers into the kitten's scruff, her manner of telling the animal to silence.

Emory's gaze went to Sorrow, went to Ama's white knuckles clutching the animal's fur. His eyes narrowed, and for a flash Ama saw how much Emory would like to kill her Sorrow.

Emory reached out with his chain-wrapped fist and gently—so gently—he pushed back Ama's hood. Cold rushed over Ama's head, into her ears. She heard a ringing sound, high and sharp, and from inside her own head.

The cold golden chain brushed Ama's cheek, along the length of her jaw, down the line of her throat.

"Please," she said again.

Emory's free hand took the leather collar, attached to the end of the chain, and drew it around Ama's neck.

It fit her tight, but fit, it did, and he fastened the clasp so that it lay like a jewel in the soft depression where her pulse fluttered fast.

"Enough with 'please,'" Emory said, his voice still light. "Now, say 'thank you.'"

Fabiana's King

By the time they neared the castle's entrance, Ama had stopped pleading for Emory to take her off the leash. Her own hands could undo the buckle, that was true, but though that thought passed fleetingly through Ama's mind, she dismissed it immediately, though she could not say quite why.

The first person to see her in this state of humiliation—other than Pawlin, who had chortled like it was the funniest thing—was an old man sweeping the stone path outside the castle's side entrance. He looked up when he heard them coming, and his eyes went wide at the sight of them—Emory in the lead, the leash in his hand, Ama two steps behind, hurrying to keep up with the quick pace he set, the squirming lynx in her arms. Then he cast his eyes down quickly, as if he had seen something shameful, or private, and dropped to a deep bow as they passed.

The kitchen bustled, full of preparations for dinner, and Ama felt, in her arms, Sorrow straining toward all the savory smells. She tried to keep her eyes on the floor as Emory wove a path through the cooks and kitchen girls, all of whom stopped what they were doing, stirring pots, stoking fires, chopping vegetables, to drop into curtsies and say reverently, "My king."

No one mentioned Ama's current situation, of course, and more than that, no one even acknowledged her presence. It was so much as though she was invisible that Ama began to question her very existence—was she there, truly, on a leash, following King Emory through the castle kitchen? Or was she still abed, dreaming? Or perhaps she was somewhere else—somewhere farther away, and higher, much higher, somewhere thick with warmth and shine?

She was here, in this kitchen, on this chain. Her eyes glanced up and tangled with the gaze of the girl who brought her morning tray—the one Tillie had called Fabiana. Like the man outside, Fabiana's first expression was wide-eyed; but then her expression shifted, and as she curtsied deeply, Ama sensed something akin to triumph in her voice as she said, "*My* king."

All through the castle, Ama followed Emory, through the great hall and up the two sets of stairs and down the long stone hallway to the door to her very own chamber. Emory turned the door's knob and pushed it open without a moment's hesitation, as he owned this room as surely as he owned the rest of the castle.

There was Tillie, on her knees before the fire, a bucket of ashes at her side. She was filling the fireplace with fresh wood and kindling, and at this sight the tears that had stung Ama's eyes began to spill.

"I return to you your lady," Emory said jovially, thrusting the leash's handle in Tillie's direction.

Tillie stood, wiping her hands on her apron, and dropped a curtsy. "King Emory," she said.

He thrust the handle again toward Tillie, who, after a moment's hesitation, stepped forward to accept it.

Then Emory turned to Ama, his beautiful wide teeth exposed in a beautiful smile.

"No tears, Ama," he said, wiping them gently from her cheeks. "That was just fun and games, after all." And then he took her chin in his hand and drew her close, and kissed her forehead as if she were a child, and then he went away, at last.

When the door closed behind him, Ama released the choked sob she'd held in her throat all that time. She sank to her knees on the floor, set Sorrow down, and cried as if she were, indeed, a child.

Swiftly, Tillie sank down beside her and unfastened the collar from Ama's throat. "Lady," she said, her tone almost reverent. "Oh, lady."

It was the gentleness of her voice that undid Ama completely. She slumped into Tillie's arms, allowed the girl to guide her head against her chest, and lost herself in Tillie's embrace.

Ama cried, and Tillie rocked her, and Sorrow came to comfort Ama, as well, butting the crown of her head again and again against Ama's hands.

But one cannot cry forever. After a time, Ama sucked in air, and straightened herself up, and wiped her eyes with her hands. Tillie got up and went to fetch her a handkerchief, and with that Ama dried her dripping nose.

"Oh, Tillie," she said, when she was able to speak again, "it was awful."

"I can imagine it was, lady," Tillie said.

Ama shook her head, remembering everything.

"Perhaps it was just for fun," Tillie suggested.

"It was not fun for me," Ama answered.

"No," said Tillie. "Clearly not." She stood, rather awkwardly, waiting for Ama to stand, and so Ama stood.

This seemed to relieve Tillie, this return to normalcy. She unfastened the cloak's broach and laid the cloak aside. "Would you like something to drink, lady?" she offered.

"No, Tillie, thank you." Ama found her way to the chair by the unlit fire. "Could you perhaps get this going?"

"It was meant for this evening," Tillie answered, "when it is cooler." But when Ama didn't respond, Tillie said quickly, "Of course, lady. At once."

She lit the fire. She fixed a pot of barley tea and poured Ama a cup of it, and Ama held it with both hands.

Then Tillie bustled around the room, shaking out the cloak and hanging it back in its place, kneeling at Ama's feet to unbuckle her leather overshoes, then taking a brush to them to clean away dirt.

"Tillie," Ama said, "sit and have a cup of tea with me."

Tillie stopped, midstroke, brush in the air. "Oh, lady," she said, "I couldn't."

"I insist," Ama said, and after a moment more, Tillie set aside the shoes and the brush, poured herself a cup of the barley tea, and pulled a footstool up close to Ama and the fire.

They drank their tea. When Ama's cup was empty, Tillie refilled it, and when Tillie's was nearly dry, Ama reached for the pot to serve her.

"Oh, lady, no," Tillie said, covering her cup with her hand. "Thanks to you, but you should not be serving me."

Ama could have pressed, but she could see how uncomfortable Tillie was, the way she sat on the very front edge of the footstool, like an anxious little bird who was apt to fly away at any moment.

She withdrew her hand from the teapot, but after a moment she said, "Please, Tillie, help yourself to more."

Tillie looked unsure about what she was supposed to do next, but at last she grinned, a real smile, and said, "Well, lady, if you insist." She still would not let Ama pour for her, though.

Ama did not want Tillie to move from her seat beside the fire. She didn't want to be alone.

Ama gasped.

"Lady?" said Tillie. "Are you all right?"

Ama stared into the fire and did not answer. She did not want Tillie to leave. She did not want to be alone. This was something, like her knowledge that she had never before heard music, that was a fresh, new thing, something she had no memory of, from before.

Before Emory had saved her from the dragon, Ama had never been lonely.

Ama's Question

Sleep came for Ama in two parts: the first, after retiring from an uncomfortable meal in the great hall, where revelers and musicians were not enough to distract Ama from what had occurred that morning in the garden. Everyone, all up and down the table, and even the servants, looked at her with knowing eyes and whispered to one another behind their hands.

Her shame darkened her cheeks and caused her to cast down her eyes, but the queen mother said to her, "They will talk. They will always talk. It is your duty to hold your head up and not give them more to discuss than they may already have."

Ama listened, and lifted her chin.

"And *you,*" the queen mother said in a low hiss, wagging her fork at Emory as if he were a boy who had been caught stealing cream from the pitcher, "you should know better than to treat Ama in such a fashion. As if she were a scullery maid and not your future queen!"

He was pretending to look contrite, Ama saw. He was not sorry, not really.

"Ama knows it was but a game," he said. "She is not angry."

The queen mother raised one eyebrow. "She does not look *happy*," she said.

And so Ama arranged her face into a pleasant mask, whether to please the court or the queen mother or King Emory, she did not know. Certainly, it was not to please herself.

"You will have to show her you are sorry with a gift," the queen mother said. "And you, Ama, must visit me in my chambers on the morrow. We have much to discuss, you and I."

It was this that troubled Ama late in the night, after first sleep, after the warming stones in her bed had lost all their heat, but before Tillie had come to replace them. The queen mother wished Ama to visit. And so Ama would.

Would this be her life? A long, uncertain chain of answering when called upon?

Certainly not, thought Ama, rolling onto her side and taking care not to disturb Sorrow, who liked to sleep as if she were a person, head on the bolster beside Ama's, the rest of her tucked warmly beneath the cover. When she was queen, Ama thought, then her life would be surer. Certainly no one—not even the king—would dare to hurt the queen.

She told herself this, but she did not believe it. And now she was wide-awake, despite the desperate darkness of the room.

Soon Tillie would come. She would take the cold stones away and replace them with hot ones, and she would rebuild the fire, as well, if Ama asked her to.

And soon—though not soon enough for Ama—Tillie did come.

Through the thick bed curtains that surrounded her, Ama could not make out even a hint of Tillie's shape, but she knew it was Tillie in her chamber from the sound of her steps—light, even, quick.

Tillie pulled back the curtain at the foot of the bed, preparing to take the cold stones away, and her eyes widened when she saw, by the light of the candle she held, Ama sitting up in her bed. "You are awake, lady!" Her candle sent wavering shadows to dance on the walls all around.

"I am," said Ama.

Tillie came to the head of the bed, pulled back the curtain there, and placed the candle on a table near the headboard.

"Do you thirst?" she asked, after she had taken away the cold stones and replaced them with hot stones from the fire.

"No," said Ama.

"Do you need to use the pot?"

"No," said Ama, again.

Tillie made to draw the curtains closed again. "Well," she said, "peaceful dreams to you."

"Wait," said Ama. "Don't go."

There was a look on Tillie's face, just a flash of an expression—irritation, perhaps?—but she smoothed it as surely as she had smoothed the wrinkles from the blanket. "Of course, lady," she answered, and stood near the head of Ama's bed, awaiting further instructions.

But Ama did not wish to instruct her. What she wished was that Tillie *wanted* to stay. What she wished was that Tillie was her friend.

"Would you care to sit on the bed with me?" Ama asked, but for this Tillie seemed to have no answer. Her mouth opened and then closed again, soundlessly. "Sit on the bed with me," Ama said, rephrasing her question into a command.

Tillie obeyed, perching on the edge of Ama's bed much as she had earlier perched on the edge of the footstool, prepared to rise in an instant if called upon to do so.

"Not like that," Ama said, seating herself even higher on her bolsters and crossing her legs beneath the covers. "Like this."

With an air of reluctant acceptance, Tillie scooted farther on the mattress, kicked her shoes away, and folded her legs beneath her. Sorrow slept throughout the whole procedure.

A question occurred to Ama. "Tillie," she said, "where do you sleep?"

"In the servants' quarters, on a pallet," Tillie answered promptly.

"Is it comfortable?" Ama asked.

"It serves," Tillie said.

"You sleep with others, then," Ama said.

"I do."

Ama considered this. Her feeling of loneliness, and the way it contrasted with her memory of the absence of that emotion, ballooned in her chest, creating a great inward pressure. "Is it nice to be so much with others?"

"It can be," Tillie answered. She leaned back a bit onto her hands, relaxing. "There's always some girl or other with a story or a joke to tell. And when I wake between sleeps, there is almost always someone else awake, too. On a cold night, there are bodies with whom to share heat."

Ama nodded, imagining a room full of pallets, each with a girl upon it.

"Of course, it has its drawbacks," Tillie said, growing more conversational with the passing minutes. "Like when one of the girls gets a midnight guest and the rest of us have to lie still, pretending to be asleep. Why, not long ago, Fabiana—"

But then she cut off suddenly, as if she had remembered to whom she was speaking.

Ama pressed gently. "Fabiana? She is one of the kitchen maids, yes?"

Tillie nodded. "Yes, lady."

Ama remembered the glares she had gotten from Fabiana, the particular weight Fabiana had given to her words that morning.

"Fabiana, I think, does not like me much," Ama said.

"Pay her no mind, that one," Tillie said. "She is just jealous, and fancies herself more important than she is."

"Her midnight guest," Ama began, "that wouldn't be King Emory, would it?"

Tillie coughed suddenly, and in the candle's dim light Ama could see from her wide eyes, casting about, how uncomfortable the question had made her.

"It's perfectly fine with me," Ama said quickly, in an attempt to lessen Tillie's discomfort. "I don't mind at all that Emory has visited Fabiana. It's only that I wonder . . . well, that is to say . . . if she is jealous of me, as you say, does that mean that she . . . enjoys it? His . . . visiting?"

Tillie barked a sudden laugh. "From the sounds she makes, I'd say she does." As soon as the words were out, Tillie gasped and slapped her hands across her mouth. "Oh, lady," she said, jumping from the bed. "Please, I beg your pardon. I forgot my place, is all."

"Not at all," said Ama, reaching for Tillie's hand and squeezing it. "You answered a question, that is all. I am not angry."

Tillie searched Ama's face, and she must have seen proof there that she had not upset Ama, for her own face relaxed, her shoulders dropped a little, and she said, "Well, that is a relief, lady." She turned as if to go. "If that will be all, I should leave you to your second sleep. The queen mother expects you in the morning, she does, and you won't want to look worn out for that meeting."

Ama wanted to compel Tillie to stay longer, but clearly the girl wanted to leave. Ama bit back her sigh and said, "Yes, Tillie, thank you."

Tillie gone, and her candle with her, Ama stared blindly into the dark. She imagined Emory and Fabiana. She pictured his mouth on her face, on her breasts, as they had been on Ama, and she imagined his fingers parting Fabiana between her legs, as they had parted her. She wondered what Fabiana felt inside her flesh, if she truly did feel pleasure beneath Emory's hands and body.

Was it like the pleasure she felt from the warm press of Sorrow's sleeping form, up against her side? Was it equal to the pleasure of a good meal eaten? Or the relief of moving one's bowels? Or could it possibly be the way Ama felt when she sat, as near as she could, to the warmth and radiance of a well-built fire?

Settling back against her bolster, Ama closed her eyes and resolved that, come the morning, she would find out.

The King's Yard

The kitchen was crowded.

Ama had risen early, before Tillie had come to her, and had left Sorrow tucked in bed. She'd thrown her cloak across her shoulders and drew on a pair of silk slippers before leaving her room and clicking closed the door behind her.

I am not leaving the castle, Ama told herself to quiet her pounding heart. *The king could not be angry about me just wandering inside the castle walls.*

Feeling rather like a thief, Ama stole down the stairs and found her way to the steamy heart of the castle. There, in the kitchen, fires were alight in several places—under a great oven, cooking bread; beneath a vast pot, its mouth as wide as a doorway; in the expansive hearth, where several blackened pots hung, stewing various delights.

Two women and a boy no older than ten worked at rolling out

great slabs of dough, puffs of flour rising from their labors. A young girl stood in front of a large bowl, cracking egg after egg into it, ropy strands of membrane hanging from the broken edges of each shell. By the hearth, Ama saw Tillie's aunt Allys, bending to add some spice or salt into one of the three hanging pots. Allys looked up at Ama, her one green eye seeing her straight through.

Ama looked away. Tillie's aunt scared her, though she couldn't quite say why. Instead, she approached the girl with the eggs.

"Excuse me," she said, and the girl drew in a quick breath, startled. The egg in her hand slipped from her fingers, cracked against the table's edge, and fell to the floor, a mess of yolk and slippery membrane.

"Watch yourself, girl," barked one of the two women who worked at the dough, troubling herself to come over just long enough to slap the girl's head, hard, across her ear.

The girl's head snapped to the side, and she grimaced, but she did not cry out, maintaining the air of practiced acceptance of someone well used to such treatment.

"Forgive her, lady." The baker who had struck the girl bowed. "How can I serve you?"

Ama glared at the woman. "You could serve me well by going back to your work and leaving this child alone."

The baker's eyes widened, and she made a short curtsy before backing away. "Forgive me, lady," she said, as if it had been Ama's ear she boxed and not the child's.

When the baker was gone, Ama said to the girl, who had knelt and was mopping up the egg, "I am sorry I got you into trouble."

"'Tis nothing," the girl answered, rising, and remembered her manners with a curtsy, the egg-soaked rag still in her hand.

"I am looking for Fabiana," Ama said. "Have you seen her?"

The girl nodded. "She is in the larder, counting stock."

"I see," said Ama, but she had no notion of where the larder was.

The girl waved her in the direction of a far door, and Ama thanked her.

She walked quickly across the kitchen, remembering to hold her head high, as the queen mother had advised her to do, ignoring the questioning aura of everyone in the kitchen.

Then she found herself in the larder's doorway, and she stopped abruptly, blinking into the sudden darkness as her eyes adjusted. At last she could see her surroundings, though dimly—the bundles of spices hanging from the ceiling, the shelves of dried meats, the baskets of root vegetables, the heavy bags of flour.

And there, way in the back of the larder, was the body of a woman—unmoving, collapsed upon the floor.

Stunned, Ama took a moment to find her legs, but when she did, she rushed forward and dropped to her knees beside the fallen figure. Fabiana—if it was, indeed, Fabiana—lay on her side, her back to Ama, her face obscured in shadow. Ama's hand hesitated, then dropped to Fabiana's shoulder and shook it.

A garbled sound came from Fabiana, and she stirred, batting

away Ama's hand. "A quick nap," she slurred in her half sleep. "Leave me be."

Ama sat back on her heels. Just sleeping, then. She wondered if maybe she should tiptoe away and leave Fabiana to her rest, but the nagging question of why the girl was already so tired at this early hour moved her hand forward once again.

This time, she shook Fabiana's shoulder hard.

"You cunt," Fabiana said, awake now, and she rolled over and sat up in one movement. Then she saw who had awakened her. The expression on her face—mouth widened into an O, her eyes huge—made Ama laugh in spite of herself.

"Lady," Fabiana said. "I thought you were someone else."

"Yes," Ama answered. "That much I gathered."

Fabiana made to stand up, but Ama stopped her with a hand on her arm. "Wait," she said. "I want to ask you something."

Fabiana stayed as she had been bidden to do. Her white head scarf was askew from sleep, and dark tendrils of hair escaped from it prettily.

It was no wonder that Emory liked this girl, Ama thought. Embarrassed as she was, she posed the question she had come to ask. "I know that King Emory has . . . visited you," she began.

A smirk spread across Fabiana's face, bringing a blush to Ama's cheeks. "'Tis my pleasure to please my king," Fabiana answered.

"Is it?" said Ama.

Fabiana's brow gathered, confused.

"I mean to say," said Ama, "and I am genuinely interested to know the truth, if you would be so generous as to answer me . . ."

"Answer what?" said Fabiana, and her tone, belligerent though it was, encouraged Ama forward.

"Is it truly your pleasure? To please the king?"

There was another moment of confusion before Fabiana's face cleared. "Do I like it, you mean? When the king climbs me?"

"Yes," breathed Ama, relieved. "Do you enjoy it?"

"Who would not?" Fabiana said. "To be measured by the king's yard is a pleasure and a privilege, both."

"But," struggled Ama, "what is the pleasure? I mean to say . . . what does it *feel* like?"

"The king's yard? Or the pleasure it gives?"

Ama appreciated Fabiana's plain talk. "Both," she said.

"Well, for the first, it feels all different ways. It can be a soft lump of warm dough, a handful of wrinkles and weight. And then it becomes a great thick horn, like the well-cooked leg of a turkey. And then, down betwixt my legs, it feels like . . . well, a key, perhaps, or a poker to a fire. It stirs me up. It takes me apart. It makes me feel myself like a lump of warm, moist dough."

She raised an eyebrow at Ama's clear discomfort. "Is that what you wanted to hear?"

Ama cleared her throat. "Yes," she said. "I suppose." Then she said, "You know, I am to marry the king."

Fabiana's expression turned like sour milk. "And you have come to tell me to stay away from my king."

"No," said Ama quickly. "You misunderstand."

Now Fabiana tilted her head, listening.

"It is clear you find a pleasure with the king that I am well sure I am not capable of," Ama said, searching for the right words. "I thought that, perhaps, when it came to . . . well, when it came to the king's yard, you and I could have an understanding."

"What sort of understanding?"

"Well, I imagine that I will have some duties I will not be able to avoid," Ama continued. "But, as you seem to take pleasure in that which I will most likely just endure, I wanted to let you know that it would not be against my wishes if you continued to . . . take visits from the king."

There. She had said it.

Fabiana blinked at her. "Lady," she said finally, "you are greatly mistaken if you think it matters one whit whether I find pleasure or pain with my king's yard, or, for that matter, whether or not you do. What matters, only, is my king's pleasure. You, and I, and whichever other girls take his fancy, we are all servants to that."

She stood up, tucked the loose, dark tendrils of hair beneath her head scarf, and ran her hands down her skirt to smooth it. "Lady," she said, with a look of pity so unmistakable that Ama cast her gaze down from it, "if you cannot find pleasure with my king, I suggest you at least find a way to *appear* to do so. Otherwise, you risk his wrath. And a man's wrath can be mightier by far than his yard."

FIVE

The Queen Mother's Chambers

When she returned to her room, Ama found an anxious Tillie waiting for her. She was pacing the floor, with Sorrow shadowing her, pacing as well.

"*There* you are," Tillie said, her voice sharp.

"Am I not permitted to leave this room?" Ama heard her voice answering Tillie's sharpness.

Tillie bowed her head. "Of course, lady, you are free to go as you please. I beg your pardon."

Ama softened. "No, 'tis I should apologize to you. I have kept you waiting here, and I am sure you have better things to do than wait for an errant mistress to return."

Tillie looked as if she might ask where Ama had been, but instead she said, "The queen mother has requested that your meeting be over breakfast, in her chambers. I am here to dress you."

Ama swallowed. She was not hungry, and she still had no desire to visit the queen mother's rooms. But she understood that a request is not always a request, and so she allowed Tillie to dress her.

Tillie chose the red gown that Ama had worn the first night she came to the castle, and Ama made her body obliging as Tillie tended to it. Then Tillie's clever fingers braided black velvet ribbons into Ama's hair, and she knelt to help Ama fit her feet into matching black slippers.

The whole of her ministrations felt hurried and tinged with anxiety, of words unspoken, and so, at last, when Tillie had declared Ama ready, Ama took Tillie's hands up in hers and said, "I want to ask something of you. All right?"

Tillie nodded. "Anything, lady."

It was Tillie's duty to serve Ama, Ama reminded herself. As much as Ama would have liked for it to be true, Tillie was not her friend. Can there be friendship between a servant and a mistress? She did not know. "Tillie," she said, "I'd like for you to be honest with me."

"Yes, lady," Tillie answered. "About what?"

"About everything," Ama answered. "I am new to this place, as you know. I am new to everything. I have no knowledge of who I was before I woke in the king's arms. I have no idea how this world of yours works, or how I fit into it. I have only the nagging fear that I do not fit here, not really, and I am unsure which parts of myself I must carve away in order to fit the way I am supposed to. Does that make sense to you, Tillie?"

"It does," said Tillie. "That is the way of being a woman, to carve away at herself, to fit herself to the task, but, also, to be able to carve herself in a different way, when a different shape is needed."

Tillie shaped herself in service of Ama, Ama knew. In what other shapes must Tillie carve herself when she was in other parts of her day? Ama did not know anything about what Tillie was, aside from her servant.

And here Ama was, asking Tillie to carve herself further into the image Ama would find useful, a shape that may not even be safe for Tillie to assume: that of divine truth teller, guide to Ama's blindness. Why should she think that Tillie would relish such a task?

"Tillie," she said, "I was wrong to ask. Your duties are to dress me and maintain my room. I shall not ask more of you."

Tillie's face softened, clearly relieved. "You look beautiful, lady," she said. "The queen mother will be so pleased to see you."

Which was, Ama understood, Tillie's manner of telling her that it was time for her to go.

Tillie escorted Ama through the castle to the queen mother's chambers. Sorrow was left behind, in Ama's room, happily lapping a bowl of still-warm milk. When they reached the queen mother's rooms, Tillie knocked at the door for Ama, waited for the queen mother's call of "Enter," and then turned the knob and pushed the door inward for Ama to pass inside. She crossed the threshold, and Tillie curtsied and shut the door, leaving Ama there.

Ah, the room was warm—deliciously, delightfully warm. Ama's gaze flitted around the chamber, overcome by the glut of richness. Giant tapestries of floral and ivy masked the stone walls; the floor was spread thick with furs and finely woven rugs. Unlike Ama's chamber, which was large but all of one level, here the floor was terraced into several platforms—the lowest, with the queen mother's enormous fireplace, brightly burning, the second, with a dining table large enough for six, and the third, with a massive four-poster bed, roped with silks and velvet, drenched in furs and satins.

The queen mother sat to the right of her fireplace in a chair nearly as impressive as a throne, her feet up on a wide footstool. Ama saw there was another chair, across from the queen mother, slightly smaller, but angled, as well, toward the voluminous heat that poured from the licking red flames.

"Dear heart," the queen mother said. She gestured for Ama to come closer. Ama obeyed. The queen mother's chair, padded and upholstered in shiny brocade, black at its base and woven through with thick golden filigree of leaves and flowers, rose high behind her head. Two cats perched there, on the back of the chair, both black with milky green eyes that followed Ama as she drew closer.

On the queen mother's lap rested another cat, this one an enormous gray-and-black tabby, whose ferocious purr rumbled like contained thunder. The queen mother's ring-encrusted hand stroked the tabby's back in long, smooth, continuous passes, almost hypnotizing to watch.

More cats curled on pillows near the queen mother's feet. Even more cats hunched over bowls of food, devouring morsels of meat in gravy.

And mingled with the smell of the meat and gravy was another scent—the acidic biting odor of cat urine.

"Sit," the queen mother said, but there in the seat of the opposite chair was yet another cat, this one small and orangey red. Ama picked him up, and he stretched and yawned, his barbed pink tongue arching out from between his small sharp teeth.

Ama sat and, unsure what to do with the cat, arranged him onto her lap. His front paws kneaded at her skirt, claws extending and retracting and extending again, and then he circled, wound his tail across his neck, and fell back asleep.

"He likes you," the queen mother said, sounding pleased.

"He's a lovely cat," Ama said. "They all are."

"Yes," purred the queen mother with satisfaction. "My pets are the most beautiful, most well-loved, most well-tended cats in all the land. In all the *world,* most likely. You know," she continued, "when I first came to the castle, I inherited the cats that had belonged to the queen mother before me. My favorite was a small gray kitten with a white face and blue eyes. I called her Finch, because she was quick and shy like a bird. That cat was my best comfort, Ama, in my early days here. In my early *years,* even, as I adjusted to becoming a wife and a queen. She is long dead, that cat, but I miss her still, to this day."

Ama looked carefully into the queen mother's dark eyes. The woman before her was the only person who shared Ama's past—a rescue from a dragon; a voyage to this castle; a marriage to a king. Ama listened.

"Here is the truth," the queen mother said, and Ama felt herself go straight in her chair, felt her spine tingle, felt the hairs on her body stand on end. "It is a king's world in which we find ourselves, Ama. A woman, you see, is a vessel. And it is a vessel's duty to be filled. What is a cup without wine? What is a vase without flowers? A cup, you might say, is not a cup at all, until it has felt the flow of wine within it. A vase without an arrangement of blooms to hold? Not a vase, at all, really. A vase is meant to be filled. Am I making sense, so far?"

Ama's every nerve vibrated with the desire to stand up, shout loudly, and run away, away from the urine-tinged air of the queen mother's sultry-hot chambers, away from the words the queen mother spoke. But she held her nerves together, and she softened her hand, which had gripped, clawlike, in the ginger cat's fur, and she said, "I am listening, Queen Mother."

"Good," the queen mother responded. "Listen more. Because, Ama, you are no ordinary woman. You are a damsel, rescued from a dragon, and destined for a king. As I was, and as your future son's wife will be, as well."

Her future son's wife. Her future son. A chill ran across Ama's skin and her palms were slick with sweat.

"And you will be a vase that will hold the most precious, the rarest flower of all—the son of my son, the future king. You *are* important, Ama. You are special, for you alone can bear the prince to come. No one else. Only you. Only the king can plant the seed, and only you can grow it. It is a unique privilege. A unique duty. To create a king! What more, dear girl, could a damsel hope for?"

"But Queen Mother," Ama asked, managing to keep the tremor from her voice, "surely we are more than just the men we serve. What were we, before we were taken by dragons? Before we were rescued by men?"

"That is a dangerous question, dear heart," the queen mother said. "It is better, I think, if rather than asking questions—rather than traipsing about the castle, bothering the servants, for instance, at their work—"

And here, Ama could not stop her face from showing her astonishment, her cheeks from darkening with shame. How could the queen mother know that she had been in the kitchens this morning? But, of course, the queen mother must make it her business to know everything.

"—Rather than such antics, Ama, your time could be much better spent learning how to please your king, and preparing yourself for the wedding, and practicing ease in this body of yours. This life of yours. Acceptance, Ama. That is woman's greatest strength, you know. The power to accept that which must fill her."

The queen mother blurred in Ama's tears, and Ama looked down at the cat in her lap. He smiled a bit in contented sleep, wanting for nothing, questioning nothing. Two tears dropped from her eyes and splashed into his ginger fur.

"You seem to have taken well to that cat," the queen mother said. "It will be my pleasure to gift him to you."

Ama sniffed and willed herself to smile. "You are generous, Queen Mother, but I think that my Sorrow may not take kindly to another animal in my quarters. I would hate for any harm to come to one of your cats because of my Sorrow."

"Oh," said the queen mother, waving a hand as if to clear that foolish notion from the air, "I wouldn't worry about that. The king knows that your animal is not fit for the court. I would not be surprised if, by the time you return to your room, you find that problem taken care of already."

Ama's Prayer

How could she sit through breakfast, then? How could she smile and nod and make pleasant conversation? How could she drink barley tea?

She could not. Ama stood, quickly, and the ginger cat yowled as he rolled from her skirts, landed on his feet, and stalked disdainfully away. Perhaps it was the result of standing so quickly, and in such heat. Perhaps it was due to the sweet-spice tang mixed with the acidic sting of cat urine. Perhaps it was because of the queen mother's words about Emory and Sorrow. Whatever the cause, the result was that when Ama stood, the world around her seemed to narrow inward to a tiny point of searing light, so bright as to blind, so small as to almost disappear.

Ama lost connection to the places where her body intersected with the world: where her feet touched the ground, where her head existed in relation to the rest of the room. Jolted from her skin, that was the sensation—and the queen mother's words—*practicing ease in this body of yours*—screeched loudly not in her ears, for she had no ears, not in her head, for her head was gone, but in the wide great darkness of everything that was not that one bright point of light.

She caught herself before she fell, and the queen mother's chambers rushed back in with a *whoosh*—the fire, the cats, the queen mother herself—and without a word to excuse herself, Ama ran for the door, fumbled with the handle, jerked the door open, and stumbled across the threshold.

He wouldn't, Ama told herself, skirts bunched in her fists as she ran quick as she could down the halls.

He *couldn't,* Ama prayed, rounding a corner and rushing up a set of stairs.

She tried to remember the route that Tillie had taken, tried to retrace her steps back to her room, back to Sorrow, but the castle felt infinitely labyrinthine, almost as if it were alive and mocked her by moving its doors and twisting its hallways.

She would find the room. Through force of will, she would *make* the hallway take her where she needed to go. On and on she ran, panicked, undone. A painful stitch burned Ama's side, just below her left breast, but she did not slow. A stone in the cobbled floor—just a hair higher than its brothers—caught the tip of Ama's toe, and down she fell, her palms scraping against the rough grout that held the stones in place.

She pulled herself back to her feet and pushed back her hair, spilling now from her braid. Where was she? Which direction was she facing? Was she a story too high, or too low?

She would never find her way back. She was too late, she felt in her bones, too late, and too far away, and anyway, too powerless to save the lynx kitten. She hadn't saved the kitten's mother; if anything, she had been the cause of her death. And now the kitten would die too, because Ama had showed it too much affection.

Everything was her blame. Too stupid to find her way back to her room. Too effusive with her emotions. Too inquisitive with the kitchen girl. She was too much and not enough, both in the same instant. Too big and too small; too bright and too dull; too affectionate and not affectionate enough.

I'll be less, Ama promised, though to whom, she didn't know. *Just spare Sorrow, let me keep her, and I will be as small as you want me to be.*

Was she praying to a god? To Emory? Ama did not know, and, in any case, she did not think anyone was listening.

She was alone in a hallway in a castle that was not her home. She was alone in the world, in a body that did not belong to her.

A boy no older than ten came around the corner just then, carrying a large stack of linens, too heavy for his thin arms. His eyes barely peered over the top of the stack, but they widened when they spied Ama.

"Milady," he said, and he bowed, as he had surely been taught to do, causing the mountain of linens to spill from his arms in an avalanche of fabric. "Oh!" he cried. "Oh no!"

"Please," said Ama as the boy dropped to his knees and began frantically repiling his spilled linens, "I am the queen-in-waiting, and I must return to my room, at once. I have lost my way. Can you take me there?"

The boy looked up, his eyes wide with panic as he scanned the hallway, searching, no doubt, for someone who might help him, and also someone who might punish him. But there was no one other than him and Ama. She could see the boy fighting a silent battle—weighing his duty to the linens against his duty to his future queen—and it took not more than a moment before he stood, abandoning the linens and his lesser duty to them, and said obediently, "Of course, milady. I shall take you there."

Perhaps there would be a cost to the boy, Ama thought with a stab of guilt as sharp as the cramp in her side. But she could speak for him later, after she had found her Sorrow safe in her room. She would send word with Tillie that the boy was not to be punished for abandoning his chores, she promised herself.

The boy navigated the castle's hallways with the practiced surety of one who had spent a lifetime among them, and Ama followed close at his heels. It was but minutes before he had led her directly to her chamber, gesturing to her door with an elaborate flourish that could have been funny, had circumstances been different than this.

"Thank you," Ama gasped, still grasping the pain in her side.

She pushed open her door. "Sorrow," she called, and she scanned the chamber within—there, her fire, nearly dead; there, her bed, neatly made, curtains tied open, bolsters fluffed; there, her cloak and gowns and other finery; there, the ovular mirror and her own horror-struck reflection—

For, save for her mirror image, Ama was alone, alone, entirely alone.

She dropped to the floor as the linens had, just as shapeless and just as white, and her lips parted in a keening wail.

Behind her, frightened, the serving boy backed quietly away, and then he turned and ran.

The Bird's Creance

Minutes passed, and nothing changed, save for Ama. She quelled her cries and willed her hands to steady. Perhaps it was not yet too late. Maybe if she went to Emory and pleaded with him, perhaps then he would spare the lynx. Maybe if she gave him something he wanted—and here she remembered how he had come to her, in her bed—maybe, then, he would give her back her Sorrow.

Ama stumbled to her feet. She was at the door to her room before she realized that she had no idea where Emory slept, or how to find him. This realization weakened her legs afresh, and Ama may have dropped to her knees again but for her hand on the doorknob.

She heard the rustle of skirts and the soft, fast footfalls of a woman running, and then Tillie appeared.

"Lady," said Tillie, breathless, dropping a curtsy in the hallway outside Ama's chamber door. "Lady, forgive me."

"Where is she?" Ama asked. Her voice trembled like her knees.

"Lady, the king himself came to take her. Please, lady, let us go into your room. Let me make you some barley tea, let me loosen your stays—"

"Where is my Sorrow?" Ama forced herself to keep her voice steady. She wiped her hand angrily across her cheeks to dry them.

"Lady," said Tillie, "perhaps it is for the best. That animal would soon have grown much too large to keep as a pet. She was no lap cat, lady. She was a wild beast."

Tillie was speaking as if Sorrow were dead. She could not be dead.

"Where is the king?" Ama said. "Tell me where the king has taken her."

"I do not *know*, lady," Tillie said, her voice going higher and higher. "Please, lady, come inside your room." Tillie blocked the doorway, preventing Ama's leaving.

"Move," Ama said, but Tillie did not.

Ama raised her hands and pushed, hard, on Tillie's chest, knocking her backward and into the hall. Tillie made a little sound, a surprised *oof*, as she stumbled out of the doorway. Her path now free, Ama yearned to run, but she knew not if she should turn up the hall or down it. Neither choice was better than the other; she had no notion of where the king might be. She did not know where his chambers were. She did not know where he might have taken the lynx. She did not know anything.

That was not true. She knew he loved Pawlin well. She knew he sometimes visited Fabiana. It was not much—but it was not nothing.

Tillie stood in the hallway outside of Ama's chamber, and she called, "Lady! Please, lady!"

Ama ignored her, gathered her skirts into her hands, and ran.

"Fabiana!" Ama yelled, rushing into the kitchen. She cast desperately about, looking for the sly face, the straight back, the full breasts of the girl she needed.

There—standing lazily by an open door, gazing out into the gray, drizzly day. Ama could tell it was her from the set of her spine, the square of her shoulders, and the dark black curls, tied up close at the nape of her neck.

Ama pushed through the kitchen staff, who looked at her with a mix of surprise and alarm, but who tripped over themselves to back out of her way.

"Fabiana," Ama said again, grabbing the girl's arm. "Where did the king take my lynx?"

In spite of Ama's loud words, strong grip, and urgent tone, Fabiana took her time to turn around. She looked at Ama leisurely, and then said, "Your *what?*"

"My lynx," Ama repeated. Her heart struck her ribs with such force as to bruise her from the inside. "My cat."

Fabiana blinked. Then, slowly, "You think my king keeps me apprised of his every movement? You think he bothers to let me know his plans and actions?" She barked a mean laugh and folded her arms beneath her breasts, pushing them up even higher. "I come when my king calls for me. I go when my king orders it. What kind of power do you think I have?"

Ama did not waste time responding to a question she didn't have the answer for.

Pawlin, then, she thought, forgetting Fabiana and pushing past her, stepping onto the stone threshold and out into the rain.

The pebbled path away from the castle was a punishment in Ama's light silk slippers, but she did not slow her pace. And though she hurried, she knew not where she went, only that she must go, she must *do something*.

There was the old man who had witnessed her humiliation the day before. He stood now, broom in hand, under the protection of a wooden arbor, waiting for the rain to pass. Ama went to him.

She was marked as of the castle by the rich velvet of her gown, and even before she drew near she could tell from the way his eyes widened and then dropped, respectfully, that he knew her station. At once, he himself stepped into the rain, which was growing heavier by the moment, to accede the arbor's shelter to Ama.

Not bothering with niceties, Ama blurted, "I need to find the king. If not him, Pawlin."

His mouth opened and closed, but words failed to emerge.

"At *once*," Ama added with what must have sounded like authority to the man, for now he managed words.

"Milady, the falconer spends the mornings with his birds. On fine days, he hunts. On days like this, he works with them in the mews." He raised his hand—mottled, thick-knuckled, crooked—and pointed into the rain. "There."

The rain pounded now against the earth, sending up splashes of mud that darkened the hem of Ama's gown. She left the arbor's shelter, running again, her muddy skirt heavy in her hands, her fine black slippers soaked through and ruined.

"Careful, lady," called the old man from behind her—whether about the slippery path or dangers ahead, Ama could not know.

The rain was torrential now. The building Ama ran toward seemed as insubstantial as a shadow. As she ran, head tucked to chin, gown soaked through and heavy, Ama heard in her head, *Sorrow, Sorrow, Sorrow.*

There. Ama was under the awning of the mews. She shook the water from her eyes and swept her hair back from her face. Someone was inside the building, singing.

She stepped through the wide, open central doorway and found herself between two long rows of enclosures. In each enclosure perched a bird, and as she walked down the hallway that divided the two rows, the birds turned their heads to watch her go by.

It was Pawlin who was singing, a low, sweet, gentle tune. He sat at the far end of the mews, his back to Ama. He sang a song without words, only sounds that rose and fell in an unhurried, meandering pace. And, drawing closer, Ama saw that there was something, swaddled like a babe in his lap, to which he was tending.

His left hand held the bundle, and his right hand drew up, up, until the hair-thin needle in its fingers glinted in the light of a candle lit nearby.

"What are you doing?"

"Shh," Pawlin answered, without looking up from his work.

Ama stepped even closer, terrified by what she would find in his lap but knowing she must see what it was.

It was a bird. Not Isolda, one much smaller, and plainer, dark gray. Ama's breath caught as she saw what Pawlin was doing, as he lowered the needle back down to the bird's face and used it to pierce the bird's lower eyelid, then the upper eyelid, knitting them together with a thin, long string of silk.

"You're sewing closed that bird's eyes!" Ama felt her stomach roil with sick.

"I am," Pawlin said, attention on his work, voice perfectly quiet and calm. "And you may stay while I do so if you can control your tone. You are upsetting my bird."

She was upsetting the bird? Her impulse was to grab it from Pawlin's lap and throw it into the sky, to free it from its master, but so many things conspired against this plan—the wicked rain; its sewn-shut eyes; her own need to find Sorrow, regardless of the cost.

And so, she waited, watching Pawlin finish what he had started, digging the crescents of her fingernails into her palms each time the needle poked again at the bird's eyelids, each time another stitch further shuttered the bird's vision.

At last, Pawlin was done. He carried the bird to one of the enclosures, unwrapped it from the length of linen in which he had held it captive, and placed it lovingly on its perch.

Blinded, the bird sat perfectly still. Pawlin closed the enclosure gate and turned to Ama with a smile.

"Where is Sorrow?" she demanded, hiding her shaking hands in the folds of her gown.

"What I was doing just then is called seeling," Pawlin explained. "It is done with newly caught birds to minimize their stress. You see, *I* know the bird is in no danger, but the *bird* cannot know that, and so remains in a constant state of alarm until it is tamed, looking everywhere for threats. So, by eliminating the bird's sight in this way—temporarily, of course—I am sparing it from unnecessary stress." He grinned, a lock of his hair flopping charmingly across his brow. "It's kinder this way, to shield lesser animals from that which they cannot control, don't you think?"

"Where is Sorrow?" Ama repeated. Her fingers twisted now in the cloth of her gown, squeezing water from it that she imagined, briefly, as blood.

"It's no easy task, breaking a raptor," Pawlin continued, his voice gently conversational. He folded the length of linen neatly and placed it upon a shelf. "After trapping and seeling comes manning. I have always liked that word—*manning*. It means to work with the bird to get her used to her new surroundings. To help her accept that the hand that shall provide her food will be the hand of her master. To help her learn that, though she began from a place of fear, she can move into a place of acceptance and, eventually, even a place of love. My birds love me—yes, and I love them."

"Where—"

But Pawlin continued as if he hadn't heard. "When the bird accepts my hand, the stitches will be removed. Then I shall use the hood to lessen her stress, taking it off and placing it back over her head as needed. At first, each time I remove the hood, she will fly away, but I will have her tethered, of course, with a creance such as this." Pawlin lifted a long, thin leather strap from the shelf. "Rather like your leash, is it not?" he said, smiling.

"Enough of this. Where is my lynx? I demand to know."

"The bird will tire herself, flying again and again to the end of the creance, retrieved again and again by her master, replaced again and again safely on her perch, until she learns her place," Pawlin said to Ama—and then, at last, "I believe I saw our king heading toward the village before the rain began, accompanied by his steward, who, it seemed to me, carried an awkward box in his arms."

The village. Ama turned to leave the mews and spied Pawlin's cloak. Without asking permission, she grabbed it and threw it over her shoulders, pulling up its hood against the rain.

"Fly, bird," Pawlin called after Ama as she disappeared into the storm.

The Dog's Story

No one was out of doors in weather such as this, and Ama had gathered the hood of Pawlin's cloak as close as she could around her head, only peering out through the smallest slit of fabric, eyes on a spot just in front of her next step. She could see no farther than that.

From Pawlin's mews, a cobbled path led downhill toward the village. It twisted and turned, but it led reliably away from the castle, and Ama followed it.

The wide great sky, gray-black with roiling thunderheads, growled and threatened and flashed. Wind blew the rain at a treacherous angle, and Ama's skirts tangled around her legs as she pushed forward. Her whole body trembled with cold, and her fingers, purplish, clung to the soaked-through fabric of Pawlin's cloak.

She tripped and stumbled, the castle at her back, and hoped this twisted path would deliver her, somehow, to her Sorrow. It merged, at last, with a wider road—the same road, perhaps, that had carried her, upon Reynard, to the castle not so long ago—and this road led her to the village.

Rain had driven the townspeople indoors, but even ghosted, the village smells remained. Smoke, and wet ash, and human waste. Food scraps and fetid trash piles. There, the body of a small, dead dog, pushed off into the gutter, floating now in the gathering water of the storm.

How did it come to be there? Had it been a stray or someone's loved pet? Had it succumbed to sickness or the angry boot of its drunken master? It was unknowable, and now the dog's story was over, serving only as a reminder that her own beloved Sorrow could be about to meet the same fate or—worse—had met it already.

Ama was deep in the labyrinth of the village now. The main road was paved with stones, but smaller paths and alleys that branched off from it were hard-packed dirt, turned to mud in this deluge.

All around, windows were shuttered, doors were barred. Surely, Ama thought, it would be impossible to imagine that the king might be in any of these small, sad structures . . . and yet still, he *could* be. He could be anywhere. He could be doing anything. Ama blinked, and behind her eyes was the body of the waterlogged dog. She blinked again and pictured Sorrow, mewling, scratching in Emory's arms. Another blink, and the bloated dog became Sorrow, no longer fighting, but limp and bloated herself, drowned by Emory's hand.

But—no. If Emory had intended to kill Sorrow, he would not have needed to take her from Ama's room. If he wanted her dead, why not simply do it there, back at the castle? He would not have needed to do it himself. He could have dispatched Pawlin to kill the lynx, or even, terrible as it was to consider, he could have told Tillie to do it, and she would have had to obey.

Ama stood in the middle of the paved road and turned in circles, hood clenched about her face, body shaking beneath it with cold. One part of her brain argued, *But Emory had said that Sorrow must be gone before the wedding, and that day is still many weeks away,* and another voice whispered, *"Before the wedding" means any time before solstice . . . and Emory never promised not to get rid of the lynx himself.*

If there was even a chance that Sorrow could be within one of these cottages, Ama had to know. She could knock on every door she saw and demand they let her in. She could search cottage by cottage until she found what she had come for.

The structures all looked the same—thatched roofs darkened by the rain to an orangey brown; wooden shutters lidding the small windows; uneven wooden planks that formed the cottages' walls, stuffed between with twigs and mud.

She had to start somewhere. She couldn't just stand here in the middle of the street. Resolved, Ama marched to the closest cottage and pounded on its door.

A moment passed. The door opened, and the small face of a

young girl, no more than seven, peered out. Smoke from the fire lit within seeped out, and the girl reeked of woodsmoke.

"Is the king inside, along with a lynx?" Ama asked.

The girl's eyes widened, and she looked past Ama into the rain, as if searching for some explanation for Ama's presence. Seeing none, she answered.

"No," the girl said.

"My thanks," Ama responded, feeling rather stupid for having asked such a question.

She turned to go.

"Are you the damsel?" asked the girl behind her.

Ama turned back around. The girl looked at her with round, dark eyes. "That is what they tell me," she replied.

"What was the dragon like?" the girl blurted, as if she could not contain her question.

Ama had no time for questions. She had a lynx to find. Still, she considered. What *had* the dragon been like? She strained to remember. There was no fear, there, inside her brain, thinking of the dragon. For just a second she squeezed her eyes tightly closed, willing herself to remember *something*, anything.

Behind her eyes, lids squeezed tight, Ama saw bright bursts of color—red, pink, green, yellow, blue. She opened her eyes.

"There were colors," she said. "I remember colors."

The girl looked at her, blinked, and gave a little smile. Then she closed the door.

All up the road Ama went, knocking on doors. Most were

answered by surprised villagers, all of whom shook their head no to Ama's question.

Some doors she knocked upon to no avail. Whether no one was home or they ignored her knock, Ama could not tell. What if it was in one of those cottages that Sorrow was hidden? The thought of perhaps being so close to her lynx without being able to see or help her made Ama feel as if she was losing her mind.

She turned down street after street, winding her way farther and farther away from the castle. It occurred to her that she had no idea how to retrace her way to the castle, no notion in the rain and the mud where was the path that would return her to the mews . . . and then it occurred to her that if the king had truly taken her Sorrow, she would not be returning to the castle. Not of her own will, at least.

Ama felt with a certain sharp clarity that there was nothing for her back at the castle. She imagined herself, for a flash, alone somewhere far away, and very warm. It felt like a blissful dream, the idea of such solitariness. She would need nothing, not a thing, not food or drink or—

But she *would* need those things, Ama's body reminded her with a violent shiver. Fuel to burn for heat. Food and drink, too. And those things, she did not have.

The deluge slowed, then stopped, but Ama was soaked all the way through, Pawlin's cloak and her dress beneath it heavy with rain. Her black slippers had been pierced by sharp-edged paving stones, and within them her feet felt like battered claws.

Ama had ceased knocking on doors as she considered her predicament, but she had continued walking. And then, there, ahead, was the wall of Harding.

Ama remembered the Eyes.

"They are considered prizes beyond measure," Emory had told her when first they had come to the wall—was that just days ago? It felt like lifetimes. He had said, "The Eyes of Harding are said to bestow fortune upon he who possesses them. Only the glassblower can form them . . . and it should go without saying that no one may take an Eye from the wall."

Ama had asked, "Will an Eye give its bearer luck?"

"Some say it does," Emory had said.

There was the wall. On its far side, the Eyes.

Ama remembered Tillie's aunt, and her wish, and how it had been granted. Not, perhaps, in the way she had hoped—but granted, just the same.

Only a desperate soul would take such a risk as to scoop out an Eye from the wall. But, Ama decided, there was no more desperate soul than she.

Ama's Wish

No one stood guard at the door. Whether this was a good omen or bad, Ama did not know. The rain had stopped. The clouds parted to reveal a cold, hard disc of sun. Droplets clinging to branches and leaves caught the sunlight, sending out thousands of tiny glittering auras.

Ama did not know if the sun's appearance was a good omen or bad, either. She tipped back the hood of Pawlin's cloak and looked around, to see if anyone would appear to stop her.

There was no one—not a single person in any direction.

Ama pulled back the bar that kept the door closed, and slowly, with a warning moan, the door swung inward, opening for her.

Ama stepped outside. She blinked and looked around.

Inside the wall, within the serpentine twists and turns of the labyrinthine town and, at its core, the labyrinthine castle, there were walls everywhere, constraints at every turn, misdirections and confusions, tightness and limitations.

Here, just on the other side of the wall, the world seemed to widen with possibility. Here, there was distance. There was the line of the horizon, so far away that it blurred. There was open air, unsullied by smoke and bodily smells and intrigue and deception.

There, far in the distance, was the hill where she and Emory had stopped, where he had first told her about the Eyes. Then, she had not had any reason not to trust him, not to take him at his word.

Could it be that so short a time had passed between that day and this? Ama felt tired to her bones, as if she were a hundred years old, though her memory's reach was shallow.

On the other side of the wall, Ama turned to see the Eyes. There they were, tucked into the wall's mortar. She ran her hand across the wall—rough and wet from the rain—and across one Eye, as well. It was smooth and cold, also wet, as if lubricated by tears. This Eye was bright blue, beautiful . . . but not the right Eye for Ama's wish.

It was crucial to match the Eye to her wish, just as the correct key is needed to open a specific lock. Ama knew this suddenly and certainly. She walked slowly along the wall, running her hand on it, stretching up and down for every Eye within her reach.

Not the green Eye. Not the violet one. Neither this one, nor that, nor the other.

She closed her own eyes, walked blindly along the wall, allowing her fingers to trail behind her as if through water, across the smooth orbits of the Eyes and the rough mortar between. She felt her way until finally—there.

She stopped, hand pressed against the wall, the cool orb of an Eye beneath her palm. It was, she knew, the right Eye for her wish.

Bring back my Sorrow, she prayed, eyes squeezed tight—and then, quickly, more careful with her words—*Bring back my Sorrow, healthy and well, for me to keep.*

Now she opened her eyes and lifted her hand. The Eye staring back at her glowed amber in the light, and Ama may well have been looking into a mirror, so much was this Eye like her own.

There were pebbles and rocks on the ground, and Ama hunted about until she found one with a sharp, pointed edge, and she used it to scrape at the mortar that glued the amber Eye into the wall.

She worked as quickly as she could. It would not do to be caught at this work; it would not do at all. Sandy mortar rained down as she dug out the Eye, trying not to think about what it would feel like if she were to be caught, if her own eye were to be dug out from her head in such a manner.

"Who left the door open?" bellowed a man's voice from the other side of the wall.

Ama stifled a gasp, hand frozen in the air, sharp-edged rock clutched tight.

"Where is the watcher?" demanded the man, but to whom, Ama

did not know. "They will have his head, the castle will, when they hear of this treason!"

Ama forced her hand back into action. She had mere moments before she was discovered. The sharp-edged rock found purchase in the mortar and crunched through it. Ama angled the rock's tip up under the amber Eye and dug, hard, begging the Eye to come loose for her.

"Anyone could have come right through," the man's voice went on, and another voice, quieter, higher, returned, "'Tis true, 'tis true."

Her knuckles scraped against the mortar, grating and bloodied, but Ama pushed harder with the stone. She felt the Eye loosen, like a child's tooth, and, heartened and terrified, she pushed harder, shimmying the rock into the growing gap, until, at last, the Eye popped out of the wall and into Ama's open, waiting hand.

No time to spare, Ama tucked the Eye under the cloak and down between her breasts inside her gown. She threw the rock she'd used for a tool as far away as she could and ran her bloody knuckles against the fabric of the cloak.

"What's this?" came the first man's voice.

"A girl?" said the second voice incredulously.

They were outside the wall now, as well, and they had seen her—what they had seen, exactly, Ama did not know.

She arranged her face and turned, eyes hooded by the cloak, to face them.

Sorrow's Cry

"Well," said the first man. He was tall, Ama saw, and slender. "What's this, here?"

"Have you seen my lynx?" Ama said. It was hard to hear her own voice over the rush of blood in her ears. Her heart, still trapped in its cage of ribs, was trying to escape from her body.

"Didn't your da ever tell you that it's not safe out here, beyond the wall? Especially for a girl," said the second man. This one was tall too, but thick, and bearded, all of which made his thin, high voice that much more off-putting.

Had Ama ever been so small, so unsure, as she was in that moment? She felt the cool orb of the Eye tucked between her breasts, the roughness of the mortar that still clung to it. If she could wish again, in a different way, would she wish instead to be away from this place, from these men, who were walking toward her now, hands loose at their sides, grinning, swaggering, tracking?

No, she would not. It was her Sorrow she wanted. And if she would need to go through these men to get to her, then that was what she would do.

"You're a lovely thing," said the first man. Up close to her now, close enough to touch, Ama saw each part that made up his face: the pleasing bronze tone of his skin; the symmetry of his brows, arched above flecked green eyes; his full, bowed lips, stretched into a smile now; his teeth, mostly even, the blackness where one was missing from the bottom row.

Ama did not respond. She stood, guarded, waiting.

"Don't you have anything to say, when a fellow gives you a compliment?" the man asked. "I said you're pretty, didn't I? What do you say to that?"

"Yes," said Ama, for she knew she was attractive; everyone she had met had told her so, from the king to the maids.

The other man, thicker, taller, with a beard he seemed to prize, so well was it groomed, scoffed, "So you think you are pretty, do you?" And, to his companion, "Quite a head on this one. Her ma never taught her a thing about modesty, you reckon, Gib?"

The man called Gib shook his head. "You're not so great," he said. "I've seen prettier. Ay, Rand? We've seen prettier by far."

Rand nodded, narrowed his eyes, took his time looking Ama up and down, as if she were not covered head to foot in a cloak, muddy as it was. As if she were naked. "The whore at the pub last week was prettier than this one," he said. "And not stuck-up about it, neither."

The men walked even closer. Ama smelled their breath, saw

the little veins, like tiny red worms, in the whites of their eyes. She stepped back. They stepped forward. She stepped back again, and felt the wall behind her.

She was trapped now between the eyes of the men in front of her and the Eyes of the wall at her back.

Pinned there by their gaze, Ama considered her choices. She did not see this ending well for her.

Above them, the sky rumbled a warning. Clouds gathered once more, and everything dimmed. A cold wind rose up, moving like fingers through the men's hair, Gib's and Rand's, both, and blowing too beneath Ama's hood, whispering to her, warning her.

But the warning did her no good; Ama already felt the danger. She had no weapons; she had no recourse. She had only this body, which they had said was both pretty and not that pretty, after all, and yet still they remained.

"Give me my space," Ama commanded, doing her best not to shrink against the wall, trying to infuse her voice with a strength she did not feel.

"*Your* space?" said Gib. "Rand, this girl seems to think that she has some claim on the air around her."

"That's funny," Rand answered, though he did not laugh. "Last I checked, no one owns the air, least of all some girl loved so little that she's allowed to roam off alone, in the rain, outside the wall."

"That's not true." Ama flared, grasping as best she could for a way out. "I am not unloved."

"That cloak is not a lady's," Rand said. "I'll bet you stole it."

This, Ama could not deny.

"A thief, too, then," said Gib. "Looks like there are a couple of lessons you need to learn."

"Lucky we came along to teach you," Rand said.

"I belong to the king!" Ama blurted, clutching closed the cloak at her throat. "I am his damsel, and if you touch me—even the least bit, even a hair—it will be *your* heads he will be having."

Gib and Rand, who had been surging forward, hesitated and rolled back on their heels. They glanced at one another, and Ama saw in their faces their doubt.

She plunged ahead. "The king took me from the dragon, and brought me to Harding, to the castle," she said. "I am to be his queen. I will warn you just one time—do not molest me, sirs. You will not live to regret it."

"I did hear the king's damsel brought with her a lynx," Rand muttered to Gib.

The men would believe her, thought Ama; they would step back. She would be safe.

But, then—"Everyone knows about that lynx," Gib said to Rand. "'Tain't a secret, after all."

"True," Rand said, considering. "If *we* know about the king's girl's pet, most likely every slut in town does, as well."

"Probably all them whores are playacting at being the damsel, don'tcha think?" scoffed Gib, and then, with a falsetto, "Ooh, look at me, I'm the damsel and this scraggy tomcat is my lynx, it is!"

Rand laughed, shoved Gib's shoulder, and then the men turned again to Ama. "No woman of the king's is out here beyond the wall," Rand said. "No girl up to any good goes past the door. It's to your own mercy if we teach you a lesson."

"To your own mercy," Gib echoed.

And they moved toward her again, eyes glinting, mouths set, minds made.

She would scream, Ama thought. She would scream and scratch and kick. Then, just as their hands were about to touch her, and as if in answer to this thought, Ama heard a familiar yowl.

Gib and Rand heard it too, for they froze and their eyes widened. Desperate, hope surging in her breast, Ama swung her gaze in a wide arc, and then—there, exploding through the still-open door, was her Sorrow.

The lynx barreled toward the men, lips curled back, and though the men raised their hands in submission, stumbled away from Ama, Sorrow did not slow. She sprang, flew through the air, striking Rand square in the chest with her paws, knocking him backward and onto the ground.

"God's balls!" said Gib, but he didn't move toward the lynx to help his friend, instead backing farther away from both the lynx and Ama.

Sorrow flexed her haunches and growled into Rand's terrified face, her teeth inches from his throat.

"Call it off, lady," begged Rand, but Ama would not.

Then, stepping through the wall, his waxed cloak beaded with water, came Emory. And, just a half pace behind, conspicuously underdressed for the weather without his cloak, was Pawlin.

"Call it off, Ama," Emory said, and Ama did not hesitate.

"Sorrow, come," she said.

The animal did not even flinch in her posture, her ears did not so much as twitch in the direction of Ama's voice. She would rip out his throat, Ama saw, and though in that moment it might feel a relief to see Rand dead, such an action would not endear the lynx to Emory, that was certain.

Ama lunged forward and grabbed Sorrow by her scruff, pulling her back and away from Rand's exposed throat.

The cat yowled and fought, but then Ama had her up in her arms, and she squeezed the lynx with the relief of reunion, and Sorrow's stiffened form softened, and her yowl turned to purrs, her great long tongue emerging to kiss Ama's face, the rough dryness of it sopping up tears Ama hadn't known she'd shed.

At her feet, Rand rolled up to his knees, and Gib knelt, too, where he stood. "My king," said Rand, his voice raspy now, his eyes cast down, "Forgive us."

And Gib said, "How could we have known?"

Emory ignored them both. "There you are, my dearest," he said, brushing past the men without even a glance. "I have found you at last."

He opened his arms, and, still holding Sorrow tight, Ama stepped into them.

The Swallow's Inn

"Shh, shh, dear one," Emory murmured into Ama's hair. "You are safe, I have you."

Against her cheek, Ama felt the rough brush of Sorrow's tongue. Around her, she felt the warm press of Emory's arms. Safe, she allowed herself to be comforted.

"The rain will come again," Emory said. "We must return you to the castle."

Ama nodded. Yes, *yes*. The castle, where she was safe, and fed, and clothed, and warm. She wanted to go back to her room, to her fire, now that she had her Sorrow returned to her. She turned to look at Pawlin and the others.

Gib and Rand stood, their eyes cast down, their hands held open in supplication. Pawlin, who looked very strange indeed without a bird upon him, scanned the wall as if he searched for something.

Ama saw his gaze land on the divot from which she had pried the Eye. He flicked a glance at Ama, smiled, and looked away—so fast that no one but she noticed.

Pawlin knew what she had done. Ama was certain of it. Would he tell the king? Or use this knowledge in some other way? Either way, Ama was not sorry. She had her Sorrow, and was tucking her beneath Pawlin's own cloak, the lynx's warm body pressing the stolen Eye into Ama's breastbone.

Come what may, Ama would not undo what she had done. She wouldn't.

Ama let herself be led by Emory back through the doorway in the wall, waited with him while Pawlin and the others followed them inside, and as Pawlin rebarred the door.

"It's your luck the king and the lynx came along when they did," Pawlin admonished Gib and Rand. "If you had touched the damsel—"

"We would never!" gasped Rand, his voice winding up even higher. "We know the damsel belongs to the king!"

"As well she does," Pawlin answered. "Now, be sharp, lads. I've an errand for you. One of you, stay and man the door. The other, find the gatekeeper. Tell him he's wanted at the castle."

Gib and Rand nodded, eager to have been assigned a task. Gib took up guard inside the door, arms crossed stoically across his chest, and Rand sprinted off toward the village.

Thunder rumbled above, loud and close. "We will not beat the rain on foot," Pawlin said to Emory. "Shall we take shelter nearby, and send for a carriage for the lady?"

"And Sorrow," Ama cut in.

"Of course, lady," Pawlin said, bowing. "No one would dream of separating you from your pet."

Ama did not have an answer for this. Had not the king himself just hours ago quite deliberately taken Sorrow from her very room? Had not Pawlin told her in his mews that the king and his steward had headed toward the village, with an awkward burden?

She mulled over these questions as she walked, flanked by Emory and Pawlin, back into the maze of the village. They stopped outside a building, this one made of brick rather than the simple wattle and daub of the houses. A wooden sign hung outside with the signum of a bird, wings spread, carved into it above the words *THE SWALLOW.*

Pawlin pulled open the door, and raucous noise and laughter poured out in a deluge. So *this* was where the villagers had been, and why the streets seemed so eerily quiet.

Feeling shy, Ama stepped inside, followed by Emory, and then Pawlin, who closed the door behind them. It took a moment for the people to notice their entry, and another moment for them to realize that the king was in their midst. The recognition seemed to spread across the crowded pub like a wave, and the crowd went quiet in fits and stammers, and then it was silent.

In her arms, Sorrow stretched restlessly, but Ama held her still.

"Good people," Emory said, "it storms outside, but in here, all is well and dry. Bring us mead and meat, and return to your revelry. I command it so."

His words seemed to break the spell under which the tightly packed pub had fallen, and voices murmured once again, though they were more subdued. The barkeep rushed out from his place behind the counter, bowing furiously, and said, "This is an honor, indeed, yes, it is! Why, the king and his queen-in-waiting, and the falconer as well! Please, come in, come in, I'll ready my finest table for you at once!" He led them to the largest table in front of the pub's one glass window where three men sat at their cups, and he brandished his towel as if to shoo off pests. "Away, away," he told them.

They got right up and, with bows and words of welcome, cleared away from the table.

The barkeep ran his towel across its wooden surface, bowed again, and said, "It will be my pleasure to serve you, I am sure!"

Emory helped Ama off with her cloak—Pawlin's cloak, actually, but none of them mentioned that—and said to the barkeep, "We are glad to be here. Do us the favor, now, of hanging this by your fire to dry and sending for a carriage to take us back to the castle after we refresh ourselves here."

"Boy!" the barkeep yelled over his shoulder as he took the dripping cape. A small, dirty face emerged from behind the bar. The child looked as if he had perhaps been just woken from a nap. "Get to the castle and fetch back a carriage for his highness. And be smart about it, you hear me?"

The boy nodded and rubbed his eyes, then headed outside. When he opened the door, Ama saw that the rain had begun again, in earnest, and it pained her to see the boy tuck his chin to his body and dart out into the cold, wet afternoon.

But she would not complain of this, or anything. Her Sorrow was safe in her lap, and Pawlin was ordering a dish of meat and a bowl of cream to be brought out along with their meal, so the lynx could eat, as well.

The barkeep bowed and scraped, and retreated to hang Pawlin's cape to dry, to fetch their food and drink.

All around, the villagers pretended to care about their own tables while sneaking glances at Ama and the king, and the lynx, too, who sat prettily on the bench beside her mistress and passed her paw across her face to clean it.

Before the food had come, Emory excused himself from the table, most likely to find the privy, Ama assumed, and she took the moment to turn to Pawlin.

"Did you follow me?" she asked. "Did you know where I was, all this day?"

Pawlin smiled, a slow, easy grin. "You could not think I would let something as valuable as the king's damsel fly untethered?"

Ama remembered the bird in the mews whose eyes Pawlin had sewed shut. She recalled the hood of which Pawlin had spoken, and the creance, as well. "No," she answered gravely. "No, you would not."

All around, the people reveled in being warm, and sheltered, and well fed, and they knocked their mugs together, and they cheered and drank with pleasure.

Emory returned to the table, and the food arrived just after. He hummed with satisfaction at the spread laid before them, at the foamy-topped mug the barkeep poured for him.

"Now, Ama," he said, pausing to drink from his mug and wipe the foam from his upper lip, "you haven't yet thanked me for rescuing your pet."

"Thanked you?" Ama asked.

"Of course! Who do you think dodged out into the rain to chase her, that naughty cat? Why, I must have tailed her for half the morning before I caught her, after she escaped your room. And look at the wounds she gave me as thanks for my rescue," he said, pushing up his sleeves to reveal long, red welts. "Really, Ama, you'll need to keep a tighter watch on your creature from now on."

Ama did not know what to say. Was she going mad? Had not Tillie told her that the king had come to Ama's room, while she had been visiting the queen mother's chambers, and taken Sorrow away? Had not Pawlin said that he had seen the king and his servant heading toward the village, carrying what could only have been the lynx? Ama shook her head to try to clear it, but nothing became clearer, nothing at all.

Could she have misunderstood? Could she have been so terribly wrong?

And . . . *from now on.* Might Emory be implying that she could keep her lynx, after all, to the wedding and beyond?

Emory was waiting for her to speak. Ama moistened her lips with a sip from her own mug. It was foamy and bitter and cool, the beverage inside, and Ama swallowed a large mouthful before answering. At last she said, "I am sorry, my king. I did not yet thank you. Indeed, you have saved me yet again, this time from heartbreak. Thank you for finding my Sorrow and returning her to me."

Emory smiled. "All is well, Ama," he said, taking another gulp of his drink. "All is well."

Was this the right time? Should she push him now? "Emory," she said, a quiver in her voice, "the queen mother suggested that perhaps you should give me a gift."

Emory laughed softly. "Girls, always wanting more," he said. "What is it you want, Ama? Jewels? Furs? A new gown?"

"Your word," Ama answered, "that I can keep my Sorrow past the wedding, if I can manage to tame her."

"Tame a beast like *that,*" Emory said, shaking his head. "A girl like *you.*"

"Perhaps Pawlin could help me," Ama blurted. She turned to him. "You can tame any beast, I am sure of it, can you not?"

"*Can* and *should* are very different things, my lady," Pawlin answered, but that was not a no.

"At least let me try," Ama said, to Emory. She was begging now.

A moment passed as Emory regarded Ama, as Ama tried her best to arrange her face, her hands, her posture, in the best possible manner, the manner that might convince Emory to give her this gift, the one thing she wanted.

At last, Emory spoke. "You may try," he said. "Most likely you shall fail, even with Pawlin's aid, but I shall not interfere. And if you manage to tame the cat to my satisfaction—then your Sorrow shall stay. You have my word."

"Oh, thank you, my king," Ama gasped. "Thank you."

The return to the castle was as easy and dry as the leave-taking had been frightening and wet. From the pub—where Emory insisted on leaving gold coins, though the barkeep had bowed and pledged that the honor was his to serve the king, no money necessary—to the warm, enclosed carriage, to the castle door, the trip was full of ease and comfort.

In the carriage, Emory himself bent down to slip off Ama's ruined slippers, his large, callused hands cradling her feet to warm them.

At the castle, the carriage took them nearly right to the entrance, and Emory took Ama up in his arms, Sorrow asleep now on her chest, and carried her easily across the threshold.

Ama found she had no desire to walk—oh, she was tired—and she let her head rest against Emory's chest as he took her through the castle and toward her room, the servants bowing and curtsying and then whispering behind them, their quiet voices so clearly full of admiration for Emory's strength and his rescue, yet again, of his damsel.

Not until they reached the door to Ama's chamber did Emory set her down, and then he did so almost with regret, as if he was sorry to be relieved of the burden of carrying her.

Tillie emerged through the doorway, curtsied to the king, and took Sorrow, who yawned and stretched upon transfer, into Ama's room.

Emory brushed Ama's hair back from her temple, took up her hands in his, and kissed them, knuckle by knuckle, ten soft sweet kisses.

"You must rest and recover from your trauma," he said, and his blue eyes held real concern when he looked up from her hands. "Exposure to weather like this is dangerous. You could catch cold and be carried off from me, and then where would I be? A king without a queen, dear one, is not much of a king at all, for a queen is both helpmeet and legacy bearer."

"I am grateful to be safe, and to have my Sorrow back," Ama said. She tried to make herself as soft and small as Emory seemed to like.

"Rest, Ama, and bring that pretty pink back to your cheeks," Emory said, smiling. "You may take supper in your room tonight, if you wish; I will give Mother your regrets."

"That is kind of you, my king," Ama said.

Then Emory came in close, very close, so that his breath warmed Ama's cheek. His left hand wound around her waist, his right took up a gentle handful of still-damp hair at the nape of Ama's neck, and he brought his mouth down to slant across Ama's.

His kiss was soft and lingering, tender as if he feared that he might break her under the weight of his caress, and Ama held herself very still, accepting his mouth and his hands.

Emory broke the kiss reluctantly, and he smiled a wide earnest smile, and then he released her. "As many times as you need my aid, dear Ama, I shall provide it."

Ama dropped her best curtsy, and she dipped her head prettily. She held the posture as long as would any suppliant, until Emory gestured for her to straighten, and then dropped another kiss, this one on her forehead. At last Emory turned to leave, well pleased, and then a thought flashed through Ama's mind, a realization that chilled her even more deeply than the rain—

This is how he likes me best . . . when I am in need of rescue.

SIX

Sorrow's Lesson

It was Emory's use of that one tiny word—*if*—that compelled Ama to hope.

That word, that *if*, inspired Ama not only to hope that her Sorrow might remain at her side, but also that perhaps her future might still unfurl into something beautiful.

If, she thought as she wandered the gardens on Emory's arm.

If, she thought as Emory tried to teach her how to shoot an arrow, as he laughed at how it wavered and fell short of the target.

If, she thought each night at supper with Emory and the queen mother, and sometimes with the hall deafeningly full of guests.

If, she thought as she endured the clucking and questions of the guests and the housemaids and even her own Tillie, who all wanted to know if she was getting enough sleep, if she was eating enough, if she knew *why* she was losing her color and her curves and the sheen to her hair, in spite of the good care she was getting, the good meat she was eating.

If, she thought at the end of each night, as Emory walked her to the door of her chamber, as he kissed her face and her mouth and her throat, as he kneaded the mounds of her breasts through the velvet and satin of her gowns (not troubled, it seemed, by her waning figure), as he pushed her up against the door, grinding his yard into her stomach.

If she could keep her Sorrow, Ama thought, latching the door to her chamber when at last Emory released her, bringing her fingertips to her swollen lips, if only, then this, then that, then everything, would be worth it.

"Submitting a creature to your will," Pawlin began. It was a fine, blue-skied afternoon one week after Sorrow's disappearance and reappearance; Pawlin and Isolda met Ama and Sorrow in the garden to train, his gloves and a leather switch discarded on a bench nearby. "The key to this is to strike the right balance of trust and fear. That, and timing. The best-trained beasts are those who are broken before they have tasted their own power. An adult hawk trapped in a net can make a fine hunter, 'tis true, but never as good as an eyas, taken from its aerie. Away from its mother, the fledgling cleaves to its master—or mistress, such as it were—and can be bent like heated metal into whatever shape the master desires."

Babes plucked from their nests, stolen from their mothers.

Creatures compared to metal, able to be formed and reformed in the image of their master. Distasteful, all of it, enough to raise the hackles on Ama's back, had she hackles to raise. She aimed to keep her expression neutral—grateful, even—as Pawlin was taking time from his day in order to help Ama craft her Sorrow into a creature who could be allowed to remain at the castle.

If Sorrow were to be allowed to stay, there were certain things that she would need to be trained away from doing, and Ama knew it. The lynx must not bite, or claw, or growl—most especially, she must not menace Emory. She must be tamed. She must be controllable. She must learn to submit to the powers greater than she, if Ama were to protect her.

And so Ama listened to Pawlin's instructions. She stood in the winter's garden where she first had met Pawlin, with Sorrow on her leash, at Ama's side. The kitten—who had grown so nicely, eating meat and drinking cream each day since coming to the castle—amused herself rolling on the garden path, batting at a large, crisp brown leaf that she'd caught as it blew across the ground.

Isolda, perched as she was on Pawlin's glove, watched the lynx disapprovingly, her downturned beak practically a sneer.

"You'll need your cat to come when called, and leave when told," Pawlin said. "You'll need a command to get her to drop something she may have picked up in her teeth. That day at the wall, Ama, when your cat did not respond to your voice—that was a bad sign, I think. Yes, a bad sign, indeed."

Ama ignored this pessimism. "She will need a command to strike, as well, will she not?"

"Oh, I do not think you'll have cause to set your beast upon anyone," Pawlin said with a dismissive laugh. "You shall never need to hunt for a meal nor protect yourself from an attacker. You shall live all your days in the castle, surrounded by your maids, protected by the guard. And you shall be wed to King Emory, who has already saved you from a dragon, from a worse threat than any here on the castle grounds. You can train her to kill rats, I am sure, if you are afraid of vermin."

There was nothing for Ama to fear, she told herself, in her life at the castle.

"The most important thing for your beast to learn, if she is to remain your companion, is to stand down. Cats can be jealous creatures. With a smaller pet, this is mere inconvenience. But your Sorrow will grow larger and stronger, and we must teach her that you are not hers alone. We must teach her *not* to interfere, *not* to . . . misinterpret." Here, Pawlin paused. He reached up with his ungloved hand and stroked Isolda, long, slow strokes, from the top of her head to the orange-tipped feathers of her tail. "The king wants very much for you to be content here, lady. And after your lynx ran out, when he saw how distraught you were over the thought that she may be lost to you . . . well, the king sees now how important your pet is to you. What a kind and gentle king, to be so concerned with your preferences!"

"Yes," Ama agreed quickly, though her voice lifted slightly, as if she were asking a question.

"And I expressed to the king, as well, how a companion animal can help to . . . ground a person, as it were. Much as, later, a child will do for you. Now," said Pawlin, transferring Isolda from his arm to a standing perch nearby, "shall we begin?"

It was a terrible afternoon. Again, and again, Pawlin stepped between Ama and Sorrow, raising his arms and walking toward Ama, this time baring his teeth, that time stomping his feet, another time at a quick pace, and then on tiptoes, like a thief. Each time Sorrow made a move to protect her—a growl, a raised hackle, a pace forward to intercede—Ama was to admonish her with the word Pawlin had given her: *Away*.

It went against all of Ama's impulses, and Sorrow's. The cat looked disturbed and confused, pacing in short bursts, her eyes trained on Ama, a low, constant sound—not quite a growl, but most surely an expression of her unhappiness—escaping from between her turned-back lips.

It made Ama feel ill, that she was training her Sorrow *not* to protect her. *Not* to come to her aid.

But it was for the lynx's own protection, Ama told herself, doing her best to ignore her sense of unease, the quickening in her stomach when Pawlin moved toward her aggressively, the twist in her gut when, each time, she told Sorrow, "Away!"

Eventually, though, the cat did learn. The first time that Sorrow did not lunge at Pawlin when he menaced Ama, he fished a piece of dry meat from his pocket and tossed it to her. She caught it midair in her teeth, her jaws snapping shut.

"Smart girl," Pawlin praised. "Now, again."

The meat was the tipping point, and from the moment Sorrow received it, her training progressed quickly. By the time the sun, cold and shiny like a coin, hung in its midday place, Sorrow had learned to ignore her intuition almost entirely.

Pawlin's pleasure at her progress was palpable; he grinned and stroked the cat, who had come to accept his hand, along with the meat, and praised her lavishly—"You smart girl, you clever girl!"

But with his growing pleasure came Ama's dimming heart.

She had her pet. Her wish had been granted. But, as Pawlin lunged at her one final time, now grabbing both her wrists in his hands, and Sorrow sat, prettily, doing nothing, waiting for her reward, it was not what Ama had managed to retain that struck her but, rather, what she had lost.

From her watching perch, Isolda preened her feathers, drawing her beak down the length of her wing. As she moved, the bells that hung from her jesses jangled softly.

Tillie's aunt had cautioned Ama to be a cat rather than a rabbit. Her wrists, freed now from Pawlin's twin grip, still felt the sting of his hands on her, as if he had left an invisible mark.

But Ama was not a cat. She was not a rabbit, either.

Ama, severed as she was from everything, even Sorrow, did not know what she was. She knew only that a pressure was building in her chest, a burbling, desperate pain, and whether it would erupt from her or drown her from within . . . well, Ama did not know that, either.

The Queen Mother's Heart

Winter's first snow came that night. Ama stood before an open window, staring out into darkness, her room's fire breathing hot at her back.

She was alone, save for Sorrow, who rested by the fire, her amber eyes watching the flickering flame, her heavy head resting on her paws. Ama herself had thrown open the glass and the shutters as well, and she placed her hands on the icy iron railing, leaning into the silent velvet of night.

It was dark as dreams. Had there ever been a moon? It did not seem possible, so black was the sky this night. In the darkness, Ama could see nothing of the snow flurries, not the whiteness, not the ice-kissed shimmers. But she felt the temperature dropping, degree by degree, as the heaviness of night and darkness and snow swirled and thickened. Though she could not see the snow, she *felt* it there.

She felt it falling, moving, like ghosts or shadows. Like premonitions, whispers from her future.

Behind her was warmth and light; ahead of her was frost and stillness and damp, heavy darkness.

Ama felt a tingling at the base of her tongue, like a taste remembered. The fine hairs at the nape of her neck rose up like Sorrow's hackles, and she felt, with powerful certainty, that there was something there, behind her—she *knew* there was, she felt it as sure as a hand upon her shoulder . . . but when she turned to see, she found only the licking flames of the fire and the curled-close shape of Sorrow in front of it.

Ama turned back to the window and held herself very still. She closed her eyes, deepening the darkness, and tried to feel the shadow hand on her shoulder once more, tried to recapture that sense of something behind her.

At first, it would not come. Only her ghost future, creeping in with the cold, luring her, ice fingers caressing her face. Nothing at her back now. But she stood still, barely breathing, waiting, reaching, willing what was behind her to connect with her again, and as the flame's heat built an aura of warmth that pressed against the length of her back, from the crown of her head, down her neck, spreading through the velvet of her gown, across her hips and buttocks, and down her legs, Ama felt the tingle once again—a sensation that she could almost grasp, if only she stood perfectly still a moment longer. It was behind her; it was her past, beckoning her.

"You'll catch your death, lady!" Tillie's voice, loud and quick, shattered the reverie Ama had half slipped into. "It's hard enough trying to keep you anywhere near healthy without you going and leaning out into the cold like that, practically *inviting* illness." Skirts swishing, she crossed the room, set down the furs she had been carrying on the edge of Ama's bed, and cranked the window shut.

The cold whispered away, along with Ama's near-memory.

"A girl such as you shouldn't get a chill," Tillie said, as if repeating an order she had been given. "A girl such as you must be watched."

"A girl such as me?" Ama asked. "What sort of girl am I?"

"A lady," Tillie said. She was spreading the heavy furs now across the bed, adding layers of weight and warmth.

"But did someone tell you that?" Ama asked. "That I should not get cold?"

"A week ago," Tillie said, "and nearly every day since. The queen mother herself. Furious, wasn't she, as if I had anything to do with it, that day when you ran out into the storm to find your lynx. You weren't gone an hour when she sent for me. I was lucky that she thrashed me just with words, that is sure, though if you had returned injured—or, heavens forbid, had not returned at all—I have no doubt that a tongue lashing would not have been the whole of my punishment. She called me twice that day. The first time, to admonish me for 'letting' you run off, she said—'useless prat,' I believe, and 'senseless git,' she called me. And after you were home abed that night, she summoned me again."

"What did she want that time?" Ama asked, ignoring the stab of guilt that she felt over having caused trouble for Tillie.

The girl paused, thinking, casting her mind back. "Let's see," she began. "After making it clear how lucky it was for me that you had been found by the king and were home safe and sound, after that, she said, 'A lady such as your mistress is not like *you*, girl. There are certain things she needs, and it is your job to provide them—heat, most of all.'" Tillie screwed shut her eyes, concentrating to recall the exact words, and when she spoke again, it was in the singsong intonation of a lesson learned well. "The queen mother told me, 'When the snow begins to fall, the queen-in-waiting must not be cold.'" Tillie nodded firmly, and then her eyes popped open, and she shrugged. "So I begged her forgiveness and promised to do my job better. To not let you run off into the cold again, for one, and to fortify your bed with even better coverings when the snow began. And tonight, here is the snow, and here are the coverings." She patted the growing pile of furs, pleased.

But Ama was no longer listening. The queen mother had said that Ama must not be cold. And though Ama had herself felt what being cold had cost her, ever since that first plunge into the icy river—the dimming of her mind, the slowing of her senses—how could the queen mother possibly have known? Ama had never mentioned this to her, or to anyone.

"Tillie," Ama said slowly, "does the queen mother always keep her rooms as warm as they were when I visited her in them?"

"Oh yes," Tillie answered. She seemed in the mood for a chat. "Always. Winter or summer, it matters not, she orders the fires burning hot in her chambers. Why, my aunt Allys told me that when the queen mother first arrived, before the night of her marriage to the king, she just grew colder and colder, she did. Nothing could truly warm her. Fires worked only to keep the frost away, no more. She grew so cold that she near died. Her heart—it beat slower and slower, they said, but who's to know the truth of that? 'Twasn't like many had cause to listen to the beating of her heart. But folks said that her heart was near frozen before the wedding. Some folks thought there would be no wedding at all, but a funeral, instead. But marry they did, and it is well believed that it was the king's kiss that heated her heart back to life. Other folks said it was more likely his yard than his kiss that warmed her, for there was a babe in her soon after, and everyone knows that nothing warms a woman like growing a child."

"And that child was . . . Emory?"

"None other," said Tillie. She was turning back the covers now, fluffing up the bolsters.

"And the queen mother had no other children," Ama said.

"Just the one," Tillie said. And then, "Same as the queen mother before her, and the queen mother before *her,* as far back as any of us can remember. 'Tis always that way—a damsel queen births a single son. That son grows to manhood, and rescues a damsel of his own, who births a single son. 'Twill be that way for you, too, lady.

And your son will be a handsome one, I'd wager! With your red hair and King Emory's blue eyes."

"A single son," Ama said softly.

"That is the way it has always been," Tillie answered.

Later, after Tillie had arranged the heating stones, helped Ama out of her gown and into her night things, then tucked up the covers and snuffed out the lamp, leaving Ama alone in the dark, Ama remembered the snow shadows outside her window.

She could not see the snow. She had not been able to hear it falling. But she knew it was there because it made the air colder, and colder, and colder still. It made the world more silent.

In spite of the potential promise of Sorrow remaining, in spite of Emory's attentions and Tillie's ministrations, her future was like the snow. Ama could sense it, not by sight, nor smell, nor sound. But by the coldness, creeping in.

Ama's Choice

After first sleep, but before second sleep descended, Ama called Tillie to light the bedside lantern.

"Do you need the pot, lady?" Tillie asked.

"No, thank you," Ama answered, and she was about to ask Tillie to build up the fire from its embers, but before she could speak, Tillie was already heading to the fireplace. Ama watched as she stacked new logs and blew air upon the embers with the bellows, coaxing flames from nearly nothing, just with patience, wood, and a little air.

Tillie worked the bellows gently to begin; too much air too fast would extinguish the embers rather than feed them. But as the first tendrils of fire burst up, licking the wood waiting to be consumed, Tillie blew the bellows harder until, with a *foomph*, the fire flamed in earnest.

Tillie went away, and Ama, propped up by bolsters, stared into the flames. Alone once more, Ama fished the Eye from where she kept it hidden, tucked into an opening in the seam of one of her bolsters. She could not have kept the Eye on her body; Tillie would have seen it there, for sure, though most likely she would not have betrayed Ama's secret. Still, it felt unfair to ask Tillie to bear the burden of what Ama had done; who knew what the punishment would be for hiding the crime of taking an Eye?

So, when she had first been returned to her room that day, soaked to the skin, after Emory had left her, as Tillie had stripped her from her gown, Ama had palmed the Eye from where she had tucked it between her breasts and had slipped it in her mouth for safekeeping.

Tillie had fussed and bustled about, asking questions that needed no answers and directing the water bearers to set the bath in front of Ama's roaring fire. When the others had left and Tillie had her back to her, Ama had gone, naked but for the length of linen in which she was wrapped, to her bed, thinking to tuck the Eye between the blankets and hope it would not be discovered. But then her glance had landed upon the bolsters and had seen the split seam on the edge of one of them—the red one—and quick as a blink, Ama had tucked the Eye inside.

Now, in the eerie hour between first and second sleep, Ama held up the Eye, the fire lighting it. It was orange-yellow like honey, and the glow of flames behind it made the Eye shine with life, as the lynx mother's eye had done before Emory had ended her with his pickax. As she knew her own eyes to shine, having seen them often enough in the oval mirror while being dressed.

Why did she keep the Eye still? After all, her wish, such as it was, had been granted—Sorrow was hers, here, safe in this room, and learning to be a pet. Pushing back the furs and the blankets, Ama rose, bare feet on cold stone, and drew closer to the fire. She squatted down on the hearth, nightdress puddling around her, and held the amber orb up to the light. She watched the way the flames played against the strings of orange and yellow within it.

The Eye was dangerous. Maybe not in and of itself—it fit neatly in the cupped palm of her hand, not much bigger than an actual, human eye—but in what it represented. In what it proved she had done. And having kept it even this long, in the days since she had scraped it from the wall, seemed foolhardy. As if she were daring the fates. Would Emory take an eye from her head if he found what she had done? She remembered again that precious word on which her whole world seemed to balance—*if*.

Slowly, silently, Ama stood from her place by the fire and walked to the window, closed tight now by Tillie's hand against the night. It was a blank black mirror, the windowpane, with the fire's light within the room and nothing but dark outside. In it, Ama saw her reflection blinking back at her. She saw her long red hair, twisted into loose braids that fell to her hips. She saw the shock-white fabric of her sleeping gown. She saw her own face, her own eyes, but a trick of the half-light showed them not amber like the Eye in her curled-closed palm, but rather black like the queen mother's.

Ama reached out and placed her hand on the window's ice-cold crank. She knew what she should do: she should open this window once more and be rid of the Eye, right now, shrouded by night and snow. She remembered Tillie's aunt, the price she had paid for her wish, and the way it had been granted—all good reasons for disposing of this Eye, and at once. But it was so lovely, refracting firelight, aglow like a tiny sun betwixt her fingers, that Ama found she did not want to let it go.

She could have cranked open her window—and she should have—in that frozen moment, when all the world around her slept, when snow softly fell. She should have flung it far into the silent, frozen night. By morning the snow would have erased it, buried the Eye deeply and well. By the time the snow melted in the spring, Ama would have long since been a queen, most likely rounded by a future king in her belly. No one would dare take an eye from a queen. Buried like that, it would be almost as if it had never happened, almost as if she had never scraped the Eye from the wall and wished upon it.

Secrets, like memories, do not disappear just because they are buried by snow or time or distance. Snow melts. The sun finishes its orbit and begins, again, where it started. Thrown or not, buried or treasured, the Eye had been plucked, and by Ama's hand. She could not unpluck it.

Slowly, slowly, Ama withdrew her hand from the window crank. As silent as snow, she left the window. She returned to her bed. She pushed the Eye deep into the innards of the red bolster, squeezing shut its seam as best she could.

Sorrow yawned and stretched as Ama climbed back under the blankets, doing her best to not disturb the lynx as she rearranged herself beneath the furs. She snuffed out the bedside lantern. The fire's dancing flames sent shadows across the far wall, and Ama made a game of picking out shapes among them.

There was a tree, branches blown in the wind.

There was a wave, blown into foam on a rocky shore.

There was a cliff, so steep and treacherous.

There, above, was a castle, rising up from the cliff as if it had grown that way.

And there, saw Ama, so tired, second sleep almost upon her—were her eyes even open anymore? Was it a shadow she saw, or a dream, or a memory?—was a creature with a wicked, sharp-spiked tail, a spine of stairs up its back, a pair of tendon-laced wings, folded in, and a large, triangular head, all rendered in shadow-smoke upon her wall.

The dragon's head slowly turned. Then, there it was—the Eye from the wall, the dragon's eye, one and the same, amber, glowing, full of promises and secrets, both.

Ama spun and fell, head over feet, lost and afraid and excited all at once, out of space and time and memory, deep into the eye of the dragon.

The Glassblower's Staff

As another week passed and snow banked up around the castle walls, Sorrow grew restless from being kept indoors. She paced back and forth, back and forth, and put her paws up on the windowsill, yowling out into the frozen world.

"It is too cold out of doors," Ama chastened her, but that was not really true—it was too cold out of doors for *Ama,* who was cold all the time now, terribly cold, no matter how close she sat to the fire, how many furs Tillie heaped upon her bed.

It was *not* too cold for Sorrow, whose coat had thickened and darkened as she grew. The tips of her ears, pointed and black, flattened now against her head, as if she did not like what Ama was telling her.

Truth was, this was the sort of weather Sorrow was made for. The giant paws, fluff tufting out between each claw and paw pad.

The mottled coat, so dense that Ama's hand completely disappeared when she pressed her fingers into it. The wound-tight energy of her, trapped here, in this room, with Ama, when it was clear that the cat yearned to run fast and hard and far.

Ama felt small and selfish.

And cold. She felt very, very cold.

The days were a pattern of dressing and eating and changing and eating again, of using the pot and climbing into and out of her bed, days that drifted by like snowflakes, as inconsequential and difficult to grasp, nearly impossible to distinguish one from the next. And as the snowdrift grew outside, Ama felt as if she herself, on the inside, was, perhaps, turning to ice. Her heart, it seemed, beat slower and slower still. Her lids grew heavy, as if invisible icicles weighted down each lash. Her breath grew slow and shallow. Even getting out of bed to go sit near the fire became an impossible chore.

Tillie's face grew more and more concerned. "You have to get up, lady," she said, on the first morning that Ama refused to rise from bed, two weeks after the first snow had fallen. "Moving around gets the blood flowing, it does. Just lying there, like that . . . well, it isn't right!"

Ama found it difficult to muster the energy to answer. "Leave me be," she said at last.

"And you've got another training session with Pawlin to get to,"

Tillie said, as if by way of enticing Ama, but Ama only repeated, "Leave me be."

Tillie obeyed. But she returned with two boys from the kitchen carrying armfuls of wood, which she ordered stacked by the fire, and she hung a kettle of herbs and water to steam. The room did warm, growing moist and fragrant as the kettle boiled, but still, Ama did not rise.

She was neither a cat nor a rabbit. She was, perhaps, a lizard, slowing near to death and waiting for winter to pass.

The next day, when Ama still refused to leave her bed, Tillie insisted. "Lady," she said, throwing back the furs and blankets, both, "you must move." She put her hands on Ama's ankles to help turn her to stand, and gasped. "Oh, lady," she said, "how can you be this cold, under all this warmth?"

Tillie's hands burned like brands on Ama's legs, jolting her, at last, awake.

"Leave me be," Ama said, grasping for the blankets.

But Tillie would not let her have them. "Up, lady," she said briskly, and so Ama obeyed.

Tillie led Ama to the fire, and there she dressed her. A thick black gown. A leather vest. Fleece-lined slippers. Hair, plaited and wound into a bun, then covered over with a head scarf pulled over Ama's ears to keep them warm.

"Something must be done to warm you through," Tillie said, more to herself than to Ama. "The queen mother warned me about letting you get too cold. I've done all I can think of!" She shook her head in frustration. And then, as if it had just that moment struck her, Tillie said, "I know where I shall take you, lady. If there is any place where you may be made warm . . ."

It was as if Ama's mind was sleeping, so little did she care where Tillie led her. Out of the room and down a hall, down a staircase, and then another, and another still.

Ama did not know how long they walked. Perhaps a minute. Perhaps an hour. Perhaps forever. They had reached the bowels of the castle now, that much was clear. Here it was dark and still. Here it was tomb-quiet. They were beneath the snow. They were buried.

Perhaps she would follow Tillie like this, obediently, for the rest of her life. It made no difference to Ama, not really: lying abed or trailing behind her serving girl. Did any of it matter? She could eat or not, sleep or not, speak or not, die or not. One was no better than the other.

But there. There, up ahead, was light. Closer, they drew.

Warmth. Even from here, still a hundred feet away, Ama felt the heat, rolling up the hall toward her. She felt her heart move, clenching and pumping, clenching and pumping, as if it wanted to know from whence the heat came.

Her steps quickened. Tillie, who had been leading, fell behind. "I knew you would like it, lady!" she called, but Ama did not answer.

At the end of the hall, a wide-open door.

Heat hissed from the room's wide mouth. Entranced, Ama

stepped through it. Waves of blissful warmth washed over her, visible waves, distorting the air around her. Ama closed her eyes and breathed it in, pulled it into her lungs, felt it rush through her chest and spread to her arms, her legs, her head. When she opened her eyes, she felt . . . clearer. Stronger. Curious.

And she saw a man, small, with wispy gray hair brushed back from his high forehead. Dressed in a heavy leather apron, he stood with an iron rod in his hand; at the end of the rod glowed a tiny sun, which he spun to keep in constant motion. He nodded at her, once, and then he crossed the room to the source of the heat: at the far wall, a massive oven, three men tall, rumbling and hissing with fire.

And he entered the fire with his rod, the blistering hot orb disappearing into the blaze within.

Still he spun, spun, spun the rod. "So," he said, glancing back at Ama. "You are the damsel, come to warm your bones."

"Yes," said Ama. "How did you know?"

"You are not the first, nor will you be the last. Come, child," he said, nodding to a chair nearby. "Sit, and watch me work, and warm yourself. It is as it should be."

Ama obeyed. Tillie did not follow; perhaps the great fire was too hot for her to stand.

Once Ama was sitting, the glassblower seemed to forget that she was in the room, turning back to his work.

Ama watched.

The glassblower took his gather of glass from the fire and rolled it along the steel surface of his worktable. He rolled and rolled, and as it became an even more perfect sphere, the glow began to fade from sunfire orange to darkest brown. Back to the fire it went, and back to the table. Fire, table, fire. Sunbright orange. Darkest brown. Orange again. It was hypnotic, the back and forth of it, the shine and fade of it, the twisting turn of it.

Warmer and warmer, Ama softened in her seat. Blood thrummed in her veins now; she felt nearly drunk on the bounty of it.

She watched as the glassblower, satisfied at last with the shape of his orb, plunged it once more into the fire before lowering his mouth to the far end of the metal shaft, blowing into it and then capping the opening with his thumb. It was as if the orb took in the breath he expelled, and as it expanded, Ama breathed in a deep, hot breath as well, felt her lungs stretch against her ribs.

And then, again. Back into the fire. Roll the sphere on the table. Heat. Blow. Roll.

Luxurious warmth. Liquid warmth. Voluminous warmth.

She was back in that dream, her hallucination from her first days with Emory. The man held the sun on his staff, and Ama yearned to reach for it, to take it in her hands. She stood and walked, trance-like, to the glassblower's table. She watched him work the glass, and it warmed her from the outside in. She felt greedy for more, and more, and more.

It was her beloved made small, the sun. She narrowed her gaze and tilted her head, burning her eyes by staring, unblinking, into its brightness. It was a tiny, riotous monster of explosive flames.

The sensation of reliving a moment she had already experienced, of stepping into a stream of memory, overwhelmed her. Here, fierce and bright, was the sun and her very own heart, manifested as one, and she loved it.

She loved the orange-red fuzz of its curve; she loved the roil and boil of its skin; she loved the explosive jets of liquid flame; she loved the quiet dance of whorls and swirls; she loved its glitter and its shine; she loved its movement and its silence. She loved the rivers of plasma, the sprays of flaming crimson, the ribbons of copper, the constantly changing, living, breathing, beating, churning, yearning orb.

"Give it to me," Ama said, looking up at the glassblower.

"What?" said the glassblower, his attention taken from his work.

"Give it to me," Ama repeated.

"Nonsense," he said. "This is not an art for a woman. Your place is beside the fire, not controlling it."

Ama's fingers itched to grab the staff from the glassblower's hands. She balled her fingers into fists. Ah, how she wished he would pass the staff to her.

"Women's art is soft," the glassblower continued. "Embroidery and needlework. Tending to children. Mending. Receiving." He finished the orb and set it on a rack to cool. "This piece will become one of the lanterns for your wedding feast," he said. "There will be twenty-one of them, as you shall be married on the twenty-first day of the month, winter solstice."

Should it disturb her that preparations for her wedding were being made without her being consulted? Perhaps. But what bothered her more was the glassblower's dismissal of her.

Ama pulled her stool closer to the fire and reseated herself. She could be patient, she told herself. She could watch and learn.

Satisfied that Ama would stay out of his way, the glassblower began work on another lantern. It was hypnotic, watching the glass spin on the rod, watching each gather grow with his blown breath, and Ama sat and watched, hands folded in her lap, as the rack filled with orb after orb, each one near-identical to the one before.

Enough time passed that the glassblower seemed to forget Ama was there, and so when she finally asked a question, he jumped a little, startled.

"I wonder," Ama said, "about the Eyes."

"Everyone wonders about the Eyes," the glassblower answered, his own eyes fixed sternly on his work once again.

"You make every Eye, do you not, for the wall?"

"I do," the glassblower said. "I have done, for fifty years. And before I did, 'twas my father's job, and his father's before that."

"And the Eyes," Ama asked. "Is it true they have the power to effect change? That is, do they really grant wishes?"

The glassblower's face glowed with the heat of the flames as he turned another orb in the fire. Enough time passed—minutes—that

Ama gave up hope that he might answer. Then, at last, "The weak wish. The strong act."

"Perhaps sometimes," she said, "the wish *is* the action."

"I am no philosopher," the old man replied.

Did it matter if the glassblower was right or wrong? Did it change anything, anything at all, if the Eyes held power real or imagined? It did not. What mattered right now was what the glassblower believed, and how Ama might mold that belief, like heat-softened glass, to fit her own desires. The weak, he said, wish. And the strong . . .

Ama pushed up once more from her perch. In three steps, she was beside the glassblower, and her hand, open, reached out. Lit by the fire within and without, Ama said, "Give me the staff." Her voice was low and steady. "Show me how to do this. How to make the glass. How to wield the fire. I command it."

The glassblower pinched tight his mouth. He had not, Ama gathered, intended for his words to incite Ama to action. Still, she was his queen-in-waiting, and that must have commanded her some respect, for, though he did so reluctantly, he handed her his instrument.

Ama's Accident

The more time Ama spent in the bowels of the castle, in front of the forging fire, the stronger she grew.

At first the glassblower did not trust Ama; he stood just behind her, a hand on her elbow as if ready to yank her away from the fire at a moment's notice, should she do something stupid, chanting, "Careful, careful!" as she spun the gather of glass on the rod, as she dipped it into the fire, pulled it out and spun it again, and again, and again.

But as her days fell into a routine—breakfast in her chamber, then down to the glassblower's rooms to stand and work by the fire, then back to her room to dress for dinner, then a heavy meal with Emory and the queen mother—the glassblower grew more comfortable, and Ama proved through her work to have a gift for the art.

True, there was a constant, needling pain that came from leaving Sorrow alone in the room. But there was pain now, too, when Ama stayed away from the fire and her work. With Sorrow, Ama ached for the glass; with the glass, Ama ached for her companion.

She had tried to pair her two loves, on her third day down in the fireroom, but the lynx had started panting as soon as they had passed the threshold, before they were even close to the great fire itself. Her pink tongue folded out of her mouth, droplets of saliva stretching from its tip; she narrowed her eyes to slits as if to keep out the hot air; a whining sound came out from her, like a single fiddle note, high and sharp.

Ama had passed her back to Tillie, who, as on the days before, had walked with Ama down to the glassblower's room, and she told the girl to return Sorrow to her chamber above. As Ama's time spent below stretched into hours, the twist of guilt she felt for abandoning her Sorrow was counterweighted by her pleasure, the stretching and uncurling of her soul.

Emory was well pleased by the shift in his bride-to-be's countenance. But though the king knew that Ama spent her days near the forging fire, the glassblower suggested that perhaps it would be best not to go into details about whether Ama was simply warming herself or actively participating in the creation of glassworks. "No need to tell *everyone* what you are doing down here," he said, practically humming, as he carefully placed Ama's newest sculpture—a silvery spray of water, like a breaking wave—onto a high shelf. "'Tis not my place to order the queen-in-waiting *not* to indulge her fancies, but neither 'tis it my place to upset Harding's social order."

Still, the regularity with which Ama's artwork disappeared from the fireroom and the talk she heard at banquet about the glassblower's sudden upsurge in creativity, combined with the growing stack of gold coins he rattled through his hands as she worked, told Ama that the elderly artisan would be in no great hurry to see her gone from his firing room.

And the compliments Ama gathered from everyone—Tillie, the queen mother, and Emory, most of all—on her rosened cheeks, the plumpness of her mouth, upturned into a smile, the comely way her breasts seemed to swell up out of her corsets, like risen bread, attested to the improvements in her health since she had begun spending time with the glassblower.

"The heat does you good," Emory murmured at her ear one night just outside her chamber door after the evening meal. Ama, as ever, stood very still as Emory breathed, hot and moist, against her ear, his hands skimming her shoulders, down her arms, across her waist, and back up to her breasts, which he took in both his hands and squeezed. "Soon I will be the one to warm you, and from the inside," he promised, before taking her bottom lip in his teeth and pulling it into his mouth, sucking there hard enough to leave it swollen.

But it was not the heat alone that was responsible for Ama's blooming health. Ama knew it was the work that did her good.

Perhaps even more than the heat, or perhaps it was the combination of them both—the constant fire, roiling and hot, and the feeling of channeling it into the creations she made each day.

Having the pieces she created soon disappear was a fair trade for the pleasure Ama had in making them, but still, when she would return to the furnace room to find her latest creation sold, it did bring a pang, each time. For Ama felt as if perhaps she was doing more than creating sculptures of glass; as the glass warmed and melted, changing shape beneath her hands and her breath, it seemed to her that she was pulling images out of her lost memory, out of her life before she was kidnapped.

A gray wave cresting into foam.

A sharp-edged tower growing from a cliff.

A garnet rose, big as her hand.

A blue-chested bird, perched on a delicate branch.

A yellow orb, round and perfect as the sun.

A series of flat green leaves, piled up haphazardly together.

Ama had never seen a green leaf since she had been rescued by Emory; it had been fall, then winter all the life she had memory of. She had never seen red roses, either, but she formed them out of heat and glass just the same. All the bright birds had flown south for the winter, and yet still Ama made them, one after the other, flocks of jewel birds, and as she created them, it was as if she heard their song. She smelled the rose's scent as she crafted red petals; she knew the whisper of wind between waxy leaves as she formed her growing piles of green foliage.

Where did these things come from? Her past? Her dreams? It felt, as she worked the glass and the fire, that she was doing more than making objects. It was as if she was forming her very self out of the flames and hot soft glass. She was, Ama thought, realizing herself—that is to say, as she worked with the glass, she was making her very self more real.

Ama made a series of vases out of pink and red and peach-toned glass. This one was tall and long; that one was shallow and wide-lipped. It was when she was working on the third such vessel, this one rimmed in clear glass, all along the outer edge, like a river, that she received her first burn.

It happened in an instant; as she blew the clear ribbing for the vessel, she misstepped, turned an ankle, and tripped. She caught herself before falling, but her instinct was to reach out and save the sculpture, cupping the molten glass in the palm of her left hand as it fell toward the slate floor.

A heat so intense as to feel freezing cold shot through her hand, and her fingers convulsed from the pain. Half a second later, the vase struck the slate, shattering into fragments, tinkling apart into shards of brilliant sharpness.

Ama stared down at her palm, where it had, for just a moment, held the fire-hot glass. Her flesh, inflamed and reddened, angry, was coated over with a thin skin of opaline glass. Ama bent her fingers, and the glass coating splintered, still attached to her skin, into a fine network of fractures. The pain, so intense a moment ago, lessened as Ama flexed and straightened her hand. The glass moved like scales.

"Just sweep up the shards and put them in that far bucket," ordered the glassblower, who heard the crash but did not see the burn. "They can be melted down again for use in something else."

His voice came to Ama's ears as if from very far away, and she did not respond immediately, still watching her glass-coated palm stretch and relax, stretch and relax, and feeling the scratching pull of memory from deep within.

At last she looked away from her hand and down to the floor. Glass shards had ricocheted out from the splintered vase at her feet, bigger pieces at the center, smaller and smaller fragments orbiting the first great crash.

The fragments were all shades of clear and peach and pinkish gray, like scales freshly scraped from a fish. Slowly, Ama knelt down among them. With her right hand, she picked up one of the bigger fragments. A candle's flame illuminated it from behind, and Ama turned the glass shard this way and that, catching light and reflecting it.

She would not melt down these fragments, she decided. Indeed, she would need many, many more of them if she were to create the image that had just come to her mind. Then, in spite of the throbbing pain in her left hand, Ama began to collect glass fragments with her right.

The King's Guests

But Ama had no time to work with the fragments she collected, for Tillie soon came to the fireroom to take her away, back to her chamber for a fitting.

Ama concealed her injured hand beneath the sleeve of her gown as she followed Tillie through the now familiar corridors and back to her room, but there was no hiding it once Tillie had loosed the stays of Ama's dress and helped her shed it.

Standing before the fire in her underthings, Ama watched Tillie's expression as she registered the ugly red welts, the melted-in sheen of glass on Ama's palm—first, the serving girl's eyes widened in surprise, and she reached out to touch Ama's hand, and then, as she realized what this burn would mean on her *own* flesh, how much trouble she would be in for allowing the queen-in-waiting to come to such harm, her mouth trembled, her fingers shook, and she drew them away.

"Oh, lady," Tillie whispered.

They were not alone this day; two others, Rohesia and Fabiana, were in attendance to help with the fitting, waiting now quietly, near the foot of Ama's bed, and their expressions were easy to read: Rohesia, shocked; Fabiana, disgusted by the disfigurement.

"You," Tillie said, turning to Rohesia, "go and fetch my aunt. Tell her to bring her medicines."

Rohesia nodded and whisked from the room, disappearing through the door and down the hall in a whisper of skirts.

"You," Tillie said to Fabiana, "help me pick away the glass."

Tillie put her hands on Ama's forearms and seated her in the chair before the fire, then took Ama's damaged hand between her two. "Oh, lady," she said, again, her voice raw with shared pain.

Ama blinked down at her hand. It did not hurt anymore—not much—and as she rotated it this way and that, the glass that had melded with her skin shimmered in the light. When she curled her fingers into a fist, the glass crackled. In a way, Ama thought, it was actually quite beautiful.

Sorrow slept as Fabiana and Tillie knelt at Ama's feet, and Tillie took a tight grip on Ama's hand. She nodded to Fabiana, who had fingernails long like pearlescent claws, and she began the work of pulling the glass away from Ama's palm, piece by piece.

Fabiana pinched the first fragment in her nails and pulled, and up it came—oh, *there* was the pain, returned to a pinpoint—and with it came a pinch of Ama's flesh, followed by a teardrop of blood.

Perhaps it was the pain. Perhaps it was the image of that glass fragment caught between Fabiana's nails. Perhaps it was the upwelling of blood. Whatever the cause, Ama swooned, suddenly dizzy, the room around her whooshing into a single spot of light, and then everything was black.

When she awoke, it was to find herself on the floor, her hand wrapped in clean white linen, Sorrow curled against her side, Fabiana gone, and Tillie and her aunt Allys staring down at her.

"You've just had a spell, is all," Tillie said, and the familiarity of her voice, the warm press of Sorrow's body (for she had moved close when Ama had fainted), the keen expression in Allys's one green eye all made Ama close her eyes again.

Tillie and Allys waited, crouched, silent, until Ama blinked her eyes open, and then they helped her to standing, gripping her tightly in case she swooned again, and set her back in her fireside chair.

"I don't know what the king will say when he sees this," Tillie worried, her gaze on Ama's bandaged hand.

"Why should he say anything at all?" Ama asked.

"Oh, lady," Tillie said, "a man does not like his woman to be scarred."

Allys said nothing. She picked up her roll of linen and her jar of balm and placed them in a drawstring bag, which she handed to Tillie. "Dress the wound fresh morning and night," she instructed. Then she nodded her head at Ama and said, "Take care, lady."

After Allys had gone, Tillie prepared a cup of barley tea and passed it to Ama. "I wish you could stay here in your room this evening," she said, "but that is not possible. The first of the wedding guests have arrived, and there is to be a feast in their honor. It is the nobleman Grant and his wife, from Outer Lessing, along with a contingency of their sons."

"A contingency?"

"Just four of them, this time," Tillie said.

"How many sons do the nobleman Grant and his wife, from Outer Lessing, have?" Ama sipped her tea and aimed to make her voice light, so as to soften the worry line between Tillie's eyes.

"Eleven," said Tillie, with a small smile. "And two daughters, though they are both long since married." She paused, and then she said, "They are the first of what promises to be a nearly endless stream of wedding guests who will be arriving now, lady. It's just a fortnight now until the nuptials. We should have spent this afternoon fitting you for your wedding gown, but instead . . ." Tillie's eyes returned to Ama's bandaged hand. Still dressed only in her undergarments, Ama could not hide it.

A knock came at the door. "A moment," Tillie said, and she retrieved Ama's dark crimson kirtle, which had the longest sleeves, and helped Ama into it.

"Enter," Tillie said when she'd finished tying the laces, and Fabiana pushed open the door.

"The queen mother expects you in her chambers," Fabiana said. Her sly expression had returned.

Tillie spat, "Did you run and tattle, you jade?"

Fabiana lifted her chin. "The queen mother deserves to know what all is happening in her castle, doesn't she?"

Fabiana left, chin still high, and Tillie sighed, rubbing the line that had reappeared between her eyes. "So, it's to the queen mother's chambers, then, before the feast," she said, perhaps to herself, perhaps to Ama; it made no difference. And then she set to the task of readying Ama.

The last thing Tillie did before sending Ama on her way was tug down on the sleeve of the gown, hiding the linen bandage beneath it.

Ama found the queen mother abed, pillows and cats all around. Her eyes were closed, her head dropped down in sleep, but the cat on her lap—small, dark—had its blue eyes wide open. They locked on Ama as she walked through the door, and its tail twitched.

When Ama looked up from the cat's eyes, she found the queen mother's eyes were open now, and as unblinking as the cat's.

"Ama." The queen mother's voice rasped. "I hear you have injured yourself, child."

"I did," Ama answered.

The queen mother's hand lifted from the bed, disturbing a tabby resting beneath it. "Come," she said, and Ama went.

Ama put her hand in the queen mother's. It was warm.

The queen mother picked loose the knot of Ama's bandage and

unwound it, then flipped her hand palm up. At the sight of the oozing wound coated over with Allys's jelly, the tight pink skin, her mouth pursed unhappily. "Did you mean for this to happen?" she asked, her eyes still on Ama's burn.

"Of course not." Ama tried to pull her hand away, but the queen mother's grip tightened.

"Speak the truth," she said.

"I do speak the truth." Ama forced her voice to be as steady as the queen mother's. "Now, release my hand."

The queen mother smiled. Slowly, her grip loosened. Ama withdrew her hand.

"Why would I *want* a burn?" Ama asked, reapplying the bandage.

"Everyone takes release somewhere," the queen mother answered.

"Well, I did not intend to burn my hand," Ama said. She was having difficulty retying the knot.

The queen mother gestured for Ama to let her help. After a moment's hesitation, Ama relented. As she tied the bandage, the queen mother said, "The queen before me—the mother to my king—they say she found her release in pain. When she first came to this castle as damsel, she was too timid to try such things. At that time, she found her release in tears. She cried every day, they say, from the day she was rescued until the day of her wedding. Then came her son, who would grow to be my husband, and when he was a babe, when her breasts flowed with milk for him, her tears dried, for a time. But in later years—after her son was big and needed her no more, for that's how it goes, that's how it's meant to go—then, she found her release in pain."

"In pain?" Ama asked.

The queen mother nodded. "First it was little things. Refusals to nourish herself. Forced wakefulness for days on end. Then, when those pains no longer hurt, she moved on to sharper things. Embroidery needles slipped beneath her nails. Corsets pulled so tight as to crack ribs. Drops of poison to cramp the stomach, to empty the bowels."

Ama's palm throbbed as if it were a little heart.

"Eventually those pains stopped hurting too, they stopped bringing her the release she craved. And so, it came to the rope, wound around the post of the bed—there, that one," the queen mother said, with a nod to the end post of her own curtained bed. "A rope knotted twice, once around the post, and once around her neck. Her final release."

Ama blinked, and it was as if she could see the dead queen swinging there, by her neck, dressed in finery and with beautiful braids, but dead, just the same.

"If not in pain," the queen mother continued, "you must be finding release somewhere else, that is certain. What have you been up to, I wonder? Your color is back, girl."

Ama remembered her glass—her gray wave, cresting into foam. Her sharp-edged tower growing from a cliff.

Her garnet rose, big as her hand.

Her blue-chested bird, perched on a delicate branch.

Her yellow orb, round and perfect as the sun—

And the queen mother read the memory on her face, the pleasure Ama felt. "As I thought," she said, and she smiled. "You have found a way, haven't you, clever girl, a way away."

"And what of you?" Ama said. Her voice sounded loud, defiant. "What is your release?"

"My cats, of course," the queen mother answered, stroking the tabby that curled at her side. The cat began to purr. "For me, it is always my cats."

It was a day that would never end, so it seemed to Ama. Before Tillie would release her for the banquet, she made a fuss over Ama's hair, tucking jewels into the braid, muttering "distraction" and "draw the eye up" over and over again.

Then, just as she was sending Ama from the room, she called her back. "The white of the bandage is too stark against the color of your gown," she said, undoing the linen and hissing with discomfort when she saw the burn again. "Best to keep your sleeve down over your hand. With luck, no one will notice."

They waited for her near the table—the nobleman Grant and his wife and their four attending sons, who bowed and curtsied and nodded and smiled, and who ate and drank and raised their glasses in a toast to her, and Ama smiled and dipped her head in acknowledgment, as she knew she must do, and she felt herself freezing inside all the night long, freezing inside a shell of pretense, of posturing and posing.

Pawlin was at the table too, sitting to Emory's right, and it was he who had felled the pheasant that was now the meat on their plates, and he entertained the table by telling the story of the hunt.

"She is ruthless, my Isolda," Pawlin said, ripping into the breast of the pheasant with his teeth. "Once she is set on her prey, there is no turning her back. Merciless. Single-minded. A true killer."

With a shiver, Ama imagined Isolda's sharp, curved beak piercing the feathers and flesh of the pheasant.

Oh, how she chafed at being at this table! How she wished she were somewhere else—down the many flights of stairs, through the twisting corridors, and back to the forging fire. Ama imagined what she might make with broken shards of glass, the thing she would make the next day, when she was free from all of *this*.

Perhaps she could have made it through the meal without her injury being noticed, had the table been sat only with men. It was the nobleman Grant's wife who gave her away.

"That is quite a burn," said the woman. She was deep into her third cup of wine, and her voice carried loud and booming across the table, cutting into the conversation that her husband and King Emory had been engaged in. "How did you manage an injury like that?" She reached across Ama's plate and grabbed her injured hand, flipped it palm up and pushed away the sleeve that had been mostly covering it, then twisted it back and forth to better see it. "'Tis gruesome, that!"

Ama yanked her hand away, but everyone nearby was now focusing on her.

"Ama," Emory said, "show me."

For a moment, Ama considered refusing him. Her eyes darted around the table and found everyone staring at her, Pawlin with a twisted smile.

Slowly, she extended her hand. Emory took it. His mouth grew tight and hard as he examined what she had done to herself.

"It is nothing," Ama said. "It barely hurts at all anymore."

"How did this happen?" Emory demanded.

"An accident," Ama said. "I was . . . watching the glassblower work, just staying warm by the fire, and I felt curious what it might be like to wield the glass myself. It was not his fault!" she added quickly. "I pushed the glassblower to let me try my hand at the fire. I am a silly girl. I was careless. It shall not happen again."

The table was stunningly silent. No one moved, or even breathed—not the servants, not the nobleman Grant or his over-loud wife or their four boorish sons—not even Ama herself, though she could feel the pressure of her held breath burning in her lungs.

"You thought to wield the fire," Emory said, his voice nearly a whisper. "Tell me, what did you try to make?"

"Only a vase, my king," Ama said, the truth, and then a lie—"for our wedding table."

Emory looked up from her hand. His blue eyes were a storm. "Only a vase, you say?"

Ama nodded.

"You, dear damsel," Emory began, and as he continued his voice swelled to match the storm in his eyes, "you do not *make* the vessels. You *are* the vessel." And with this last word—vessel—his voice filled everything. The room. The cups. The ears of every guest and servant. Ama's mouth, and stomach, and heart.

"You dare to burn the hand of my bride?" he said, his fingers tightening around Ama's. And now his voice was quiet again, and all around the table, the nobleman Grant and his wife and four attending sons leaned forward, and Ama had the distinct impression that Emory was both angry and *performing* anger, in the same breath.

"Do you mean . . . *my* hand?" Ama asked.

"Your hand does not only belong to you, Ama. I found you, I named you, I brought you here. You are my bride, and your flesh is my flesh. Do not treat it so roughly. In fact," he continued, discarding Ama's hand and lifting instead his goblet, from which he took a deep pull of wine, "it is for the best that you do not return to the glassblower's fireroom. Since you are, as you say, a silly, careless girl."

"But," Ama began. She felt heat rising in her cheeks. From shame? From anger? "But I must return," she said. "What about the vase I intend to make, for our wedding table?"

"Nonsense," Emory said. He motioned to a valet to bring him

another slice of meat. The man leaped to obey. "I am sure the glassblower will be glad to have you out of his hair. He is a busy and important man, and he can make any piece we may require for our wedding feast far better than you could hope to do. We should not have forced him to be your nursemaid even this long."

"That—" began Ama, but Emory cut her off.

"I am sure there is much for you to learn before our wedding night," he said. "But best it be learned from the castle's women. Perhaps you'd be better set alongside the kitchen hearth to keep you warm, and with the maid Fabiana as your teacher."

His grin was wide and slow, as if he thought certainly his inference would be lost on Ama.

It was not.

That seemed to be the end of it, and the guests, with evident relief, returned to their food and conversation.

"A girl can be burned just as surely at the kitchen's fire as the glassblower's," Ama said, but without any real hope of changing Emory's mind.

"Perhaps after the banquet," Emory said, leaning in close and dropping his voice so that just Ama could hear him, "you can show me how careful a girl can be." And then he smiled again, and his inference, once more, was not lost on Ama. Not lost at all.

Ama's Lessons

With the fireroom forbidden to her, Ama had no choice but to submit to the onslaught of wedding preparations, to the arranging of hair and lacing of stays that seemed to be the true backbone of her life here at the castle.

Banquets and guests and wine and spiced meats. Gowns and ribbons and slippers and braids. Chewing and sipping and swallowing, swallowing. All of it, the preparation, the repetition, the mastication, seemed absolutely meaningless to Ama.

If she were choosing—but, of course, she was not free to choose—her days would be spent in the fireroom, working at the glass, where Ama would not need fancy gowns—indeed, a place where elaborate dresses would be an undeniable detriment. She would need something simple, perhaps, to protect her tender flesh from the molten glass and fire, something not too loose so as to be a danger near the flames, but not so fitted as to constrict.

Constrict. Constrain. Conscript. Construct. Consume.

Words beat in Ama's head as her heart beat against the boning and binding of the gown in which she stood, trapped—the dress that was to be her wedding gown. It managed to be both debilitatingly loose in sleeve and train, making moving even about the room a difficulty, and uncomfortably binding, squeezing against her ribs and pushing her breasts together and up in a terribly uncomfortable fashion.

"Be still, lady," Tillie admonished through a mouthful of pins. She knelt at Ama's feet to adjust the gown's hemline, pinning it up so that just the toes of Ama's velvet slippers peeked out.

"I am trying," Ama said, and she heard the irritated snap of her words, "but how much longer will this take?"

"Longer if you move than if you submit," Tillie mumbled, doing her best to pin the hemline straight.

The girls on either side of Ama, whipstitching the arms in place, broke into tandem giggles.

Ama could not see what was so funny about her predicament, and her face must have reflected her confusion, for Tillie said, "Don't mind the girls, lady. Their minds go straight to the gutter, they do."

"Ah," Ama replied.

Behind her, Sorrow paced the room. It had been too long since last Ama had taken the cat out of doors, and Sorrow's pent-up energy roiled beneath her darkening coat, stretching her muscles and sinews, and escaped in the form of a constant, low growl.

Ama made a decision. "I will give you ten minutes more," she said to Tillie. "Then I shall take Sorrow to the gardens to train."

"We do not have time for that today," Tillie said, her eyes on her work. "And besides, it threatens to snow again soon. It is not a good day for you to go out of doors."

"Tillie," Ama said, "which of us will be queen in less than two weeks' time?"

Tillie's hands, full of pins, froze at Ama's hemline. She looked up. "You, lady. You shall be queen."

Ama nodded, once. "Ten minutes," she said.

Ama expected that going outside with Sorrow would feel like a great triumph, an escape, but the garden, too, was walled, and though Ama would have liked to run and play with the lynx, and though she unclipped the golden leash from Sorrow's collar when they reached the garden, Pawlin appeared almost as soon as they had arrived, as if he had been waiting for them, and reminded Ama that the pair of them still had work to do.

"Sorrow, come," Ama said to the lynx, who ignored her. The sky was gray in a way that felt like memory, but that only served to irritate her more. Tillie had been right about the snow—the air was heavy with the promise of it—and Ama and Sorrow would not have long in the garden before it began to fall. Ama knew that Pawlin reported each training session to Emory, and if she were to be allowed to keep the lynx, there could be no wasted time under Pawlin's watch, no failed training sessions.

But the lynx was not yet fully grown, still more kitten than cat, in demeanor if not in size, and away from the castle at last she seemed far more interested in stalking shadows than submitting to any training plans Pawlin had devised.

"Come," Ama said again, her voice higher with pleading this time.

Pawlin, leaning against the garden wall, Isolda on his shoulder, watched Ama attempt to bring the lynx to heel. "She will never listen to you if she does not respect you," he said, almost lazily. He and Isolda perched and watched and judged as Ama failed to convince Sorrow to come to her side when called. "And respect," Pawlin said, "is the twin brother of fear. The two are a pair, you see. You cannot have one without the other."

"I won't have her fearing me," Ama said through clenched teeth. She wanted Sorrow to *want* to come when called. She wanted Sorrow to *choose* obedience, if obey she must.

"Then we waste the little time we have left," Pawlin said, drawing his cloak tighter around his tall, slim form. Isolda ruffled up her feathers as if in pantomime.

"She will learn," Ama said. But she walked to Sorrow and reattached the leash to the lynx's collar, a concession she had not wanted to make.

"Only if you teach her," Pawlin chided.

Ama tugged gently at the leash. Sorrow, who had been sniffing the base of a winter-dead bush, turned her amber eyes up reprovingly. "Come, Sorrow," Ama said, doing her best to make her voice firm and authoritative.

Perhaps it worked; Sorrow left the bush and slunk to Ama's side. "Good girl," Ama praised, and began to walk the circuit around the garden, praying that Sorrow would stay close the whole way around, as Pawlin said she must.

There was no joy in this endeavor; watched and judged by Pawlin and Isolda, and sickened by the feeling that what she was doing—training a lynx to heel—went against the nature of both the animal and herself, Ama felt, as she almost always felt, that it was duty rather than pleasure moving her through this chore.

They circled past the wide trunk of the walnut tree. They rounded the stone bench. They made it three-quarters of the way down the straightaway between the far side of the garden and the wall where Pawlin leaned before Sorrow had had enough of the lesson.

She stopped walking. Just like that, she stopped. And when Ama tugged at the leash, the lynx settled her haunches into the frost-laced path and dug in her claws, as well.

She was so big now, Sorrow was. Almost too large for Ama to have any hope of controlling. Ama pulled at the leash, trying to disguise from Pawlin how hard she worked to move the creature, but Sorrow did not want to be moved, and she stubbornly resisted.

Ama felt the double gazes of Pawlin and Isolda, both judging, both coldly amused, both assessing all the ways she was failing.

What was *wrong* with this animal? Did she not know that her very ability to stay at the castle depended on Ama's ability to bring her to heel? Did she not understand that it was her duty to submit to Ama, just as it was Ama's duty to submit to Emory? And why *should* Sorrow feel as though she had any right to an opinion, or a preference, or a desire at all, for that matter?

Ama did not have such luxuries. *Ama* could not determine if she "felt" like being obedient, if she "wanted" to submit to Emory. It was her duty to perform as ordered. It was Sorrow's duty, as well, but the beast seemed obstinately unaware of this very basic fact.

"Fear and respect," drawled Pawlin. "Two pillars, I tell you!"

"I don't want her to fear me," Ama said again, but this time she spoke through gathering tears and a hard, hot lump swelling in her throat.

"Better that she fears you now than King Emory later," Pawlin said. And in his voice was something like pity, some frank offering of truth. This was the thing that broke Ama. For he was right, and Ama knew it. Better for Sorrow to fear her now than King Emory later.

"We all must listen," she told the lynx, almost pleading. "It is for our own good." Still the cat would not move. Stubborn, willful, selfish beast.

So, from a fold in her cloak, Ama withdrew the leather-wrapped switch that Pawlin had given her, and which she had sworn she would never use.

She straightened up, squared her shoulders, and her voice rang clear as a bell when she said, "Sorrow, come."

When the beast still did not move, Ama closed her eyes for half a second, opened them wide, and brought the switch down. The switch tore through the air and landed on Sorrow's flank with a loud, angry slap.

Sorrow yowled and arched her back, ears flat against her head. Then she hissed, lips pulled back, teeth flashing.

"Sorrow, come," Ama said again. She heard her own voice as if from far away. From the sound of it, she could not tell that inside her very chest, her heart was crumbling to ash.

The lynx hissed again, and narrowed her amber eyes. Then she slunk forward and came to Ama's heel.

"Good," praised Pawlin. "Well done."

He could have been praising Ama. Or, just as easily, and perhaps more likely, he could have been praising himself. For, Ama thought, as she led her Sorrow on another loop of the dead winter garden, just as the snow began to drift down from the sky, it was almost midwinter, she was almost a bride, and, like Sorrow, she was learning her lessons very well.

SEVEN

Sorrow's Collar

That was the last time Ama took Sorrow out of doors for training in the garden. That night, snow fell in earnest, like heavy wet ash, and dampened the world.

Days passed, seven of them. Sorrow languished. In the week after Ama took the whip to her, the lynx refused food, only lapping apathetically at her water dish. Her coat grew greasy and unkempt. She lay with her muzzle on the hearthrug, her amber eyes tracing embers upward as they went. Her chin, ashen from the rug, barely lifted at all. The ridge of her spine and the twin arches of her hip bones jutted out.

Emory needn't have worried about Sorrow. Ama had done for him the work of making the animal into nothing more than a listless house pet. There was no danger in her anymore. Her teeth were not used for eating, let alone attacking, and her claws, darkened by ash, would not be raised in Ama's defense.

Tillie came and went, building up the fire again and again, and Ama sat listlessly beside it, falling once more into her own dark sadness. Forbidden now from visiting the glassblower, she did not leave her room for any reason—not even to dine with the king and the onslaught of nobles arriving for the wedding.

It was accepted, Ama's self-imposed isolation; it happened this way sometimes, with damsels, in the days before the wedding, or so Ama heard from the whispers of the women who tended to her. But she did not respond. Her eyes were the only part of her that seemed to move at all; back and forth they darted, from the fire to the snow falling outside the window and back to the fire again.

Tillie pulled open Allys's drawstring bag each day, redressing the burn on Ama's left hand, but as soon as she left, Ama would wipe the balm away, leaving a greasy stain on her skirt, and stare into the glass-mottled scar as if trying to see something in it.

"Lady, please," Tillie begged each time she entered the room, this time proffering a mug of ale, that time presenting a meal, another time suggesting a change of gown, a change of venue, a change of outlook.

But Ama had already changed. She did not know where she had started, or what she had been, but she knew it was not this.

Not this, she thought, looking at her hands, one scarred, one pure.

Not this, she thought, her breaths constricted by the gowns she had to wear.

Not this, she thought, shaking her head slowly as she watched Sorrow grow thin and lank, shoulder bones jutting.

Not this, she thought, upon seeing her reflection in the silver goblet Tillie forced into her hands.

But she *did* see something in the goblet's gaze that startled her into motion. She blinked, set down the goblet roughly, its contents splashing onto the table, and strode across her room to the tall ovular mirror where she stood for all her fittings.

She stepped close as she could to the mirror and stared into the eyes reflected back.

Had her eyes always been this color? They were tawny, like chestnuts. Had they not once been lighter? More yellow? Like Sorrow's, and like the Eye she had taken from the wall?

But the eyes that blinked back at her were not amber. Decidedly not.

Ama returned to the fire and knelt by the lynx. She stroked the cat's greasy pelt, from forehead and down along her back, feeling each heartbreaking knob of the cat's spine. After a moment, Sorrow blinked open her amber eyes, then dropped them once more upon the hearthrug, as if even the effort it took to hold open her eyes was too great.

She was dying. Ama knew it. Though there were just three days remaining until Ama's wedding to Emory, Ama was certain that Sorrow would not live that long.

"Oh, Sorrow," Ama said. "My darling Sorrow." Sick of stomach but sure of what she must do, Ama rose to her feet.

"Tillie," she called, her voice strong and clear, and the girl must have been just outside her door, for she appeared at once.

"Yes, lady?"

"Find the king," Ama ordered. "Tell him I have need of him."

No one wanted Ama to leave the castle in such weather. She was delicate, they said, and in poor health. She should wait until after the wedding, at least, to venture out of doors.

But Ama insisted.

And so it was that she and Emory were bundled into a carriage heaped high with furs, and with hot stones at their feet, and Sorrow, as well.

Ama did not feel like talk as their carriage steered through the town, and Emory did not press her for conversation, for which Ama was grateful. She and he sat side by side, underneath a shared fur, and she felt the warmth of his long leg down the side of her through the layers of their clothing. Sorrow lay pressed against the door, in spite of the cold that seeped in underneath, panting.

Ama watched the cat's long needled tongue and listened to her labored breathing until she could stand it no more. And then she burst out, "It is not warm! Why does she pant?"

"It is a sign of stress in an animal," Emory answered. "It need not be warm for an animal to fear."

Ama leaned down to stroke Sorrow's head. The lynx neither

rejected nor registered this affection, her panting continuing, a ruff of her fur jutting up where her collar wound around her neck.

At last they reached the wall, and the gatekeeper—a different man than the one who had abandoned his post in the rainstorm, Ama noticed, but with disinterest—pulled back the bar to let the carriage through. But snow piled too high a mere fifty yards from the gates, where there were no peasants to clear it away after such a storm, and the horses couldn't pull them much farther. So Ama yanked open the carriage door, ignoring Emory's call—"Let me do it, Ama, you should stay inside"—and stepped out into the snow.

The drifts were knee high and dense as death. Ama's legs felt the shock of cold, and then tingled into numbness. She turned back to the carriage and lifted the lynx, who was so large now, and awkward to carry. At least the lynx was large. Perhaps her size would help her.

Then, Sorrow in her arms, Ama turned into the vast whiteness of the world beyond the wall.

Each step cost her. The snow, like hands, gripped her ankles, clawed at her skirts. Ama walked a pitifully short distance away from the carriage—no more than a few feet—before her knees trembled and she could go no farther.

Then, gently, she set Sorrow on the snow. She took the lynx's head in her hands and turned her face up so that Ama could look down into her amber eyes. She knelt, and kissed the lynx's head, and pressed her forehead against the cat's.

"Sorrow," she said, low and quiet so that only the cat could hear, "I love you. Run free, my darling. Catch rabbits. Drink from streams. Remember me, if you like. Forget me if that suits you."

Sorrow's head was up now, her eyes brighter, her nose twitching in the cold air as if she smelled delights unknowable to Ama, who reached for the clasp of the collar and, with nearly frozen fingers, managed to wrench it free.

"Sorrow is no more your name," Ama announced, her voice louder. "Now I call you Fury."

The collar slipped to the snow, nothing but rubbish, and free of it, Fury shook her thick dappled coat. She turned her head in the direction of the forest, sniffed the air once more, and was off—her first few steps a trot until she found her legs in the snow, and then she ran, loping fast and free, away from Ama, and Emory, and the carriage, and the wall, and all the things behind it.

She did not look back, not once.

Emory's Grip

Ama knelt in the snow, staring after Fury, long past the time when the lynx had disappeared into the frost-heavy trees of the forest.

It would be fine if I knelt here until I became the trees. Until I became the snow. The thought filled Ama's mind, and she felt herself growing stiller and stiller, her limbs stiffening in the cold, her eyes half frozen, gazing after her Fury, not wishing her back but wishing her on, on, away, gone.

"Ama!" called Emory from the carriage behind her. She heard him throwing back the furs, she heard the squeak of his foot on the runner.

Quickly, now, with fingers so stiff as to be nearly useless, Ama reached beneath her cloak and plunged her hand—so icy—down the bodice of her gown. She fumbled blindly, fingers too cold to feel, and heard Emory trudging through the snow.

There. Her fingers clawed at the Eye, warmed by her breasts, and plucked it out. It flashed, amber and open, all-seeing and blank at the same time. And then she closed her fingers into a fist, and it disappeared.

Emory's footsteps crunched ever closer through the snow. Quickly, now, Ama pressed her fist into the snow at her feet, only opening her fingers when they were deep buried. Then she pulled up her hand and smoothed the snow over, blanketing the Eye where it would rest until spring. Finally, she stood and turned to Emory.

"Thank you," she said, doing her best to smile, "for bringing me here, and for waiting while I said farewell."

"I told you, did I not," said Emory, his hand on Ama's elbow as he guided her back to the carriage, "that wild beasts do not make for good pets?"

"You did," Ama answered. She allowed Emory to help her into the carriage and settled back onto the seat. "You did."

Emory seated himself next to Ama, and the carriage master, who was as silent as a ghost and nearly as invisible, shut the carriage door. The horses were whipped into motion, and, as Emory pulled the furs back over their laps, the carriage took them back toward the castle.

Under the blanket, Emory's hands found Ama's. "You are half frozen," he said, and he rubbed her fingers vigorously between his palms, bringing them back to life with painful, needlelike tingling.

Ama did not cry out, not at the pain of her skin reawakening, and not at the pressure against her burned palm, either. She sat, stoic, and allowed the ministrations. The carriage jostled them back and forth as it rolled through the snow-soft town, the air heavy with the smoke of so many combined fires.

Emory rubbed and rubbed until Ama's hands were near as warm as his. And then he stopped, though he did not release her. Ama sat still, wanting nothing, wishing nothing. For all she had wanted and wished, what had it brought her?

"You know," Emory said, his voice quiet with secret, "you need not have thrown away that Eye."

Ama stiffened, and her heart seized. "My king?" she asked.

"Oh, don't be silly," Emory said, his mouth widening in a liquid grin. "Of course I know you took an Eye that day. Do you not think I know everything that happens in my kingdom?"

"You . . . saw me take it?" Ama did not bother with a lie.

"Well, no. But Pawlin saw the gap, of course, and he pointed it out to me. And why else would you have gone beyond the wall?" Emory did not wait for Ama's answer. "It matters not. You could have kept the Eye, if it gave you pleasure. You are to be my queen in three days' time, after all. No one would dare to punish you for such an infraction, not while you are under my protection."

"I see," Ama said. Emory's hands still trapped hers, and he held them in his lap, and she felt beneath the tangle of their hands the rising of the king's yard.

Ama tried to pull away, but Emory's grip remained firm. Indeed, he pressed her hands down upon the growing, hardening lump at the center of him.

"We are but three days from our wedding, Ama," Emory murmured. "I am your secret-keeper, and soon to be your husband. Surely you would not deny me a taste of your sweetness, now, this day, after the favors I have given you?"

He did not wait for an answer, and still he did not free Ama's hands. Holding them both in one of his, he managed to twist free the buttons of his trousers, and then he guided Ama's fingers to the shaft of him.

A noise like a hiss escaped from Emory as he used his hand to wrap Ama's fingers around his yard. It was hot and hard, with a dew-wet drip at its tip. Emory moved Ama's hands within his grip, up and down, up and down, slowly at first and then faster, until, with a grunt and a groan and a spasm so tight that the knuckles of Ama's fingers cracked, a jet of warmth spilled out of him and trickled down Ama's hands, still encased in Emory's.

A moment passed, during which the only sounds were Emory's labored gasps and the intermittent squeaking of carriage wheels. When Emory's breath had quieted, he cleared his throat and released Ama's hands, which were still wrapped around the king's yard, now softening and shrinking.

Her fingers were coated with the sticky mess of him. Ama pulled her hands away from Emory, still under the furs. Quietly, she rubbed away the wetness on the carriage's seat cushion as Emory adjusted himself and refastened his trousers.

Then she tucked her hands back into her lap and sat as still as she could. The carriage made its way back to the castle. Her face was blank, and her hands were still, but in her mind, Ama was imagining the lynx bounding across the unmarked snow, wild and free, farther away from the castle with every moment that passed.

The Queen Mother's Truth

Without the lynx, Ama's room felt even larger and colder than it had before. Emory had returned her to it, and at her door, he took her hand—the right hand, without the scar—and kissed it.

"I will not see you again until the wedding," he said. "It is our tradition for the groom to leave the bride in the three days before the ceremony."

"Is it?" Ama asked.

"To build an appetite," Emory answered, and he grinned.

"Ah," Ama answered.

"In the meanwhile," he continued, "since you have been obedient, and since you will no doubt be lonely without your pet, you can return with my blessing to the glassblower's fire, as long as you promise not to endanger yourself. Leave the glassblowing to the man, Ama."

"That I promise."

"Then until we meet at the altar," Emory said, and bowed, and then he left.

Ama went into her room. Tillie was there, waiting for her beside the fire. Ama could feel Tillie wanting to reach out to her. To comfort her. But the lynx was gone, and there would be no comfort for that. Only the knowledge that gone was better than here.

"I should like to go to the glassblower's room," Ama said. And then, "The king has given his permission."

"Oh, that is good, lady! The heat down there will do you such good after traveling out of doors into such cold air. Only . . . Lady, well, the queen mother has sent for you once again, you see. She said you are to go to her rooms as soon as you are returned and dry, she did."

A visit with the queen mother. Ama could think of few things more distasteful, in her current mood, in her desire to return to the fires of the glassblower. But this was her lot, it seemed. To do what others wished of her. To hope to carve out only stolen moments for her own desires.

"Very well," she said. "Put me in a fresh gown, then, Tillie, and let's have it over with."

Again—or, perhaps, still—the queen mother was abed, propped up by bolsters, wrapped around in layers of fur and blanket.

Ama hesitated in the doorway, wondering if maybe she could sneak away without being seen.

But then the queen mother called, "Well, do not lurk in the door, girl, letting all the warm air out!"

And so Ama went inside and closed fast the door behind.

She approached the bed, and the half-dozen cats perched upon it fixed her in their glowing green stares. Three cats piled at the queen mother's feet; a fourth curled in her lap; another pressed tight against her left hip; and a sixth, the ginger male whom Ama had held when first she visited the queen mother's chambers, nestled in the queen mother's cradling arms, like a suckling babe.

"You wished to see me, Queen Mother?"

"Come closer," the queen mother said.

Ama did. She walked all the way across the room and up to the bottom of the queen mother's bed.

"Closer," the queen mother said, and Ama walked from the foot of the queen mother's bed to the head of it. Around the queen mother's shoulders draped a familiar fur—buff-colored, richly dappled. It was the lynx mother's pelt, made into a wrap for the queen mother. Ama looked down into the queen mother's near-black eyes, and the queen mother looked up into hers.

"Ah," said the queen mother, smiling. "So it has nearly happened, then."

Ama was about to ask what the queen mother meant, but then she remembered something that Tillie's aunt Allys had told her, the very first time they met.

"She was a beauty," Allys had said. "Ink-black hair, and shiny, it was. Eyes of amber. A figure worth rescuing, no matter the risk. Bosoms, tremendous bosoms, a waist no bigger around than the king's hands could hold. Small feet. Pretty hands."

Eyes of amber. But the queen mother's eyes were not amber now. They were dark, deep, almost black—as Ama's were becoming.

"Your eyes," Ama said. Her voice came out in a whisper.

"Yes," the queen mother said. "And yours."

Ama felt her knees weaken, and she sunk to the bed. At once, the ginger cat twisted out of the queen mother's arms and stepped prettily into Ama's lap.

"He favors you still, that one," the queen mother said, nodding at the cat. "Perhaps today you will be ready to accept my gift of him, now that your lynx has gone away."

"I set her free," Ama said, not bothering to wonder how the queen mother knew. And though her hand stroked the cat, her gaze searched the queen mother's eyes.

"It was a kindness," the queen mother said. "And, for my son's sake, I am glad to see that you are capable of such a selfless thing."

"It was not selfless," Ama said. "I could not stand to watch her die, as she would certainly have done, had I kept her here with me."

"Everyone and everything will die," the queen mother said ruthlessly. "Death is the one truth." She narrowed her dark eyes. And then, quieter, she said, "In three days' time, you shall wed the king. You shall become the queen. From this becoming, there shall be no unbecoming."

"That is not entirely true," Ama said boldly. "For you have been the queen, and now you are the queen mother. And I shall take your place, shan't I? You shall unbecome the queen."

"When I came to this castle," the queen mother said, "there was no queen for me to replace. She had ended her own story, as I told you before. Do you remember?"

The queen swinging from the bedpost. Of course Ama remembered.

"Had she lived to see me come to the castle, her story would have ended in this bed, instead of hanging from it. By the time the king had planted his seed in me, the king's mother would have died, most likely in her sleep."

The cat in Ama's lap stretched his claws, stretched and stretched, one paw and then the other, kneading himself a nest.

"This is how it has always been. We come; we are tilled and planted; we grow our crop; we wither; we die, whether by our own hand or the hand of time, it matters naught. I have been tilled. I have been planted. I have grown my crop of one good son. Now I wither; soon I die."

Ama's hand had grown still on the fur of the ginger cat.

"If you stay, I go," said the queen mother. "If you go, I stay. You will be queen in this world, and there can only be but one."

Ama's Fragments

"If I stay," Ama said. Her voice was slow.

"Of course you shall stay," the queen mother said. "The damsel always does. I stayed, after all, did I not?"

"You did," said Ama. "But what of you before the dragon? What of any of us? Could you not have left to find out?"

The queen mother shook her head. "There are but two paths from here," she said. "And the road is not one of them."

"I do not wish to die."

"Nor do I. I am dying now, you know, and I am surprised by my resistance to this fact. I suppose I have found that living quite suits me. Perhaps I could have been a good ruler. A just ruler, even. I will never have the chance, of course—this is a world for men. My husband ruled the lands, and now my son shall, as it should be. So we will not know what I could perhaps have done with real power.

You shall be queen, and helpmeet, and I shall be dead."

Ama began to protest—why should the queen mother die, just because Ama would wed her son? It was unnecessary. And though the queen mother had held no special spot in Ama's affections, the thought of her dead did not suit Ama either. Imagining the queen mother lifeless in her bed, eyes closed to the world, felt like a harbinger of Ama's own inevitable death, perhaps in the very same bed, perhaps surrounded by the grown kittens of these very cats, not so many years away.

"Queen Mother," Ama asked, "why did your eyes change from amber to coal? Why have mine?"

"Yours are not yet black," the queen mother contradicted. "You have not yet had your wedding night."

"But they will blacken," Ama said, "as yours have done."

"It is the way it has always been," the queen mother answered. "Your heart, once fire-hot, is transforming. You feel it. I know you feel it."

Ama nodded.

"And that is the way it has always been," the queen mother said again. "And if something is the way it has always been, who are we to wish it otherwise? Who are we to want anything at all? Who are we to desire?"

Unbidden, in a flash, came the image of Fury bounding through snow under a bright-blue sky.

"I desire," Ama said.

"Do you?" said the queen mother. "How interesting."

The cat had settled now. It was a heap of ginger fur, one paw twitching in sleep. "That cat favors you," the queen mother said again. "Would you like to take him now, for a pet?"

"I have no need of a pet," Ama said, placing the cat, who mewled unhappily, on the coverlet, and then standing.

"If not now, then after the wedding," the queen mother said. "They shall all be yours, all my cats, after that. Do care for them, won't you? They have been such a comfort to me."

Ama made no promises. She turned to go.

The queen mother called after her, in a tone Ama hadn't heard from her before. "Remember, Ama."

Ama stopped, stood still, waited for her to finish.

But that was all she said. "Remember."

When Ama found her way back to the glassblower's room, the heat breathed out at her in a welcome wave. She breathed it in, filled her lungs full of the fire-warmth, and felt herself melt a little.

"You return," said the glassblower, who was not working. He sat as far from the fire's mouth as he could get, sipping a drink that he held in both hands. His words were as wet as liquor.

"Indeed," Ama answered. Then, "You look uncomfortable, Master Glassblower. I imagine a day or two away from the fire would do you good."

"This is my place," the glassblower said. "There is no other."

Ama considered her position. She very much would like the glassblower to leave, but, as he said, this was his domain. She had no power to command him from it. What work she might do, she would have to do beneath his inescapable gaze. Like his Eyes surrounding the city and castle, here too he would watch her, and judge her, at his will. But, Ama decided, though she could not be rid of him, she *could* ignore him.

"Very well," she conceded. "You shall stay. But do not trouble me."

"Bah," said the glassblower.

"Where are the fragments from before?" Ama asked. "The broken shards I set aside?"

"Melted down, of course," said the glassblower. "You think I keep a barrel of scraps for no reason?"

"It was not *no* reason," Ama said, anger rising in her throat. "The reason was, I had need of them."

"Beg your pardon, lady, but even the queen-in-waiting cannot tell the glassblower how to do his work."

It would be nothing but a waste of time to argue her point. "No matter," Ama said. "I shall make more."

She took up a great glass bowl from its place on a rack, raised it a foot or so, and let it slip from her fingers.

The glassblower's protest died on his lips as the bowl shattered into pieces, some as large as her hand, others as slight as dust. He watched, openmouthed, as Ama moved on to the next piece she wanted, this one a wide rosy platter, and knocked it against the edge of the rack, splintering it into a thousand fragments.

"You have lost your mind," the glassblower said, rising.

"When I am queen," Ama said, "I shall pay you well for your lost work, and even better for your discretion."

The glassblower weighed her words for a long moment. Then he lowered himself back into his chair. "You shall pay me *very* well," he amended her promise.

"*How* well," Ama said, "will depend on how thoroughly you are able to leave me to my work."

The glassblower sipped his drink, nodded curtly, and turned his back on her. Not quite as good as leaving the room entirely, but better than nothing.

Ama looked at the shards she had made. Each was a sliver of the thing she planned to create. She would need many, many more of them.

After all, she was building a memory. Of what, she did not yet know.

Ama's Three Days

What is three days? To a young beauty in the arms of her beloved, it is a moment. Nine months later, to the woman she becomes, and gripped in labor, it is a lifetime.

Ama's three days passed in both ways at once. She fell in love and she birthed, in the same motions: in the breaking of each cup, plate, bowl, platter, and vase; in the gathering of every shard, from the tiniest to the greatest; in the melting heat of the poker taken from the fire, touched to the tips of the shards, softening and melting each one.

At first, Ama did not know what she was making, only that she must make it. The pounding in her head and in the scar on her hand beat to her the queen mother's word: *Remember. Remember. Remember.*

It began to take shape. Slow, slow, but sure.

As Ama melted together fragments and shards and little broken bits, her eyes began to see what her hands were making.

It was a great spined beast. Opaline. A triangular-tipped tail that widened to a thick root. An ovular body with four clever clawed hands. A crested neck. A high, wide forehead. A pointed snout.

It was, Ama saw, a dragon.

Each scale was a fragment of glass, each softened by fire and hardened into this, the thing Ama made in her three days.

At first the glassblower did his best to ignore her, as she had told him to do. But the days were long, and the nights still longer, and though Tillie appeared and reappeared, begging Ama to leave her work, to attend her final dress fittings, to sleep, if just for a little while, Ama worked on. The glassblower stayed, sometimes awake, sometimes asleep. Even while he dozed, Ama worked on, and each time the glassblower jolted awake, it was to find Ama still at her work, and her dragon becoming something more.

At last, the glassblower could neither ignore Ama's creation nor pretend to. He stood from his chair. He peered from behind Ama, grunting as she attached another and another glassy spine. He crept closer and closer until Ama could feel his hot, moist breath on her neck.

"If you want to be of service and not just in my way," she said finally, "you can tend the fire."

It was to his credit that the glassblower did not complain about being relegated to the assistant's role. The truth was that he wanted to see what became of Ama's three days nearly as much as she did.

And so he stoked the fire to greater heat, and when his flask was dry, he refilled it with water rather than more liquor, and as the second day rounded into a third and Ama's creation became undeniably a dragon, his grunts shifted into *aah*s of appreciation.

"'Tis nearly alive," he said, "the way it catches the fire and glows. 'Tis as though it breathes."

Ama did not look up from her work. She held a palmful of glass shards as fine as whiskers, and one by one she put the tip of each to the poker, fresh from the fire and glowing red-orange with heat, until it softened, and then she took it to the chin of the dragon, where she pressed it gently among the others, framing the dragon's mouth with tiny, knife-sharp scales.

"What about eyes?" the glassblower said. For the dragon's face was flat from forehead to snout.

"You would not show me how to make eyes," Ama said, still absorbed in her delicate work.

"That was before," the glassblower said. "Now I will show you."

It was a moment until Ama answered. Then, "No," she said. "Thank you, but no. I shall make the eyes on my own."

And when she finished with the dragon's chin, Ama took a bright-yellow chalice she had found pushed to the far back of one of the glassblower's shelves, dusty and forgotten. She dipped it in water to clear the dust away, and then she broke it neatly on the table. She gathered the pieces into a thick metal bowl and pushed the bowl into the fire, where the fragments fell in upon each other and went from solid and sharp to liquid and without beginning or end.

But the color was not quite right, Ama saw, when she retrieved the bowl from the fire and stared into the molten glass. She took a knife-sharp shard from the worktable and ran it along her finger. Red welled up, like tears, and Ama squeezed her blood into the liquid glass.

She stirred the mixture, blood deepening the yellow to honey-rich amber, and then Ama was ready to craft the dragon's eyes.

Now the glassblower had set himself back in his chair, arms loose at his sides. Ama formed the blood-glass into two orbs, and these she affixed to the face of her dragon.

She finished her work just as the sun went down on her third day, and she stepped back to admire it. The glassblower admired it too.

"It is beautiful," he said, and Ama knew it was, though she knew not what it meant. They stood together, in silent appreciation of the thing Ama had done.

And then the glassblower's door slammed open, and Emory filled the doorway.

Emory's Third Weapon

"Master Glassblower," Emory said, teeth set in a line, "give me a moment alone with my intended."

And though the glassblower had not been willing to leave his room on Ama's request, he scuttled like a beetle, through the door and away, even as Emory spoke the words.

"I have come to collect you, Ama, and take you to the altar. For it is time that you take your place at my side. I ask you, Ama—why have you not returned to your room to ready yourself for our nuptials? Surely you know that this is the night we wed?"

"I have been working," Ama said.

Emory laughed. "Working? But . . . why?"

"Look," Ama said, and she stepped to the side, revealing, behind her, the dragon she had made.

Emory's smile faded. The color from his face drained away. Ama watched his eyes dart over her glass dragon, from its amber eyes to its spike-tipped tail, down the spiny scales of its broad back, across its vast wings, folded in at its sides.

"What have you done?" he whispered.

"It came from me," Ama said. "I do not know where, or why, but, Emory, I think it is my own self trying to tell me something. I want to know more, Emory. I want you to tell me about the day you rescued me from the dragon."

"It does not matter," Emory said, his eyes still ensnared by Ama's creation.

"It *does*!" Ama's insistence rang loud. "It does matter. I must know, Emory, please. Tell me—why was I in that castle? How did I come to be trapped by the beast? Why was I unharmed when you found me? And what happened to the dragon?"

Emory's gaze snapped away from the sculpture, and to Ama. "I told you. I conquered the dragon. I rescued you from it."

"So you say." Ama grew insistent with impatience. "But . . . you conquered it *how*? You rescued me *how*?"

"Ama," said Emory. His voice had shifted, become softer, cloying. "Some things are just better for you to entrust to me. If you had need of such knowledge, surely I would have given it to you. Have you not yet learned that I have your interest at heart? Think of Sorrow. Had you but listened to me when I first said that wild beasts do not make good pets, think of how much heartache you could have saved yourself, having to learn that lesson the hard way."

Ama *did* think of the lynx. She remembered the playfulness of her, as a kitten, in that grassy field. She remembered, too, the look in the mother cat's eyes. The look of recognition that Ama would not hurt her kit, and then the look, seconds later, when the pickax had struck her.

"Had you not needlessly killed Fury's mother, I would never have taken her as a pet," Ama said. Her heart beat faster, hotter, in her chest.

"Fury?"

"That is what I call her now. She is Sorrow no more. She is Fury, and she is free."

This angered Emory, that was clear. He strode closer, until Ama felt his breath on her face. "Say another word," he threatened, "and I shall set Pawlin and Isolda after your Fury. They shall hunt her, and they shall find her, and our son shall sleep in a cradle lined in her pelt."

Now the heat of Ama's blood roared in her ears. "You would not," she said.

"Indeed I would, and I will," Emory said. As Ama heated, so Emory seemed to cool and calm, as if he believed that all of Ama's fire and anger could amount to nothing.

"I believe your time in the glassblower's presence and his humoring your desires to . . . make such things as this"—and here he waved a dismissive hand at Ama's dragon—"has filled your head with all the wrong ideas. You see, Ama, it is for men to create. It is for men to decide. It is for men to speak. It is *your* place to listen, and follow, and gestate. And those are no small things! For without women to listen, how would the men's words be heard? Without your fertile womb, how could my son hope to grow? You are important, Ama. Desperately important. But do not overreach."

"Tell me how I came to be here," Ama said. "Tell me where the dragon is."

"The dragon is gone," Emory said. "I conquered the dragon, and you should thank me well for the favor rather than being a thorn to me. Upstairs, your girl waits to dress you for the altar. The prior readies the chapel for our nuptials. The cooks in the kitchen prepare a great feast. The musicians tune their instruments. All of them wait, and for what? A girl. No more. Just a girl."

"Where is the dragon?" Ama said again. A scent—a sweet-spice tang—filled her nostrils.

"Gone!" shouted Emory, and he took his arm and slashed it into Ama's creation. It happened too fast for Ama to stop him. Her dragon shot across the table and fell to the floor, shattering into a thousand tinkling, impossible pieces.

"Gone!" Emory said again, his voice now triumphant. "Do you not see how lucky you are to be freed of that dragon? You have no idea. I saved you from a life of meaningless solitude and monstrosity. I made you beautiful and I brought you here to be a queen. You, Ama, were nothing until *I* lifted you. Until *I* took you from that place. I am a *hero,* Ama. A savior. I am a king. And I demand you treat me as such!"

But Ama did not see Emory now. She barely heard him, as if

his voice came from far away. She was in a great room, surrounded by great beauty—sculptures of jewels, collected and hoarded and transformed into carefully constructed dances of color, shape, and light, each of which told a story, called forth an emotion: Here, in citrines and diamonds, a monument to spring, and hope, and youth. There, in rubies of all shades and shapes, an angry roar and blood spilled in battle. Under a wide window, a twisting river in emeralds and sapphires, dotted with diamonds to make the water glint.

The great hall was a sanctuary; the gems, its altar.

And Emory had come to destroy it, just as he had ruined her glass dragon.

She had been the artist. She had been the dragon.

Ama looked up from her shattered glass, into Emory's face. "You," she said.

And Emory saw that she knew. He lifted his chin. "And what of it?" he said. "Without me, what would you be? A monster? I made you beautiful."

"Without you," Ama said, "I would be free."

"Oh, free," said Emory, with a wave of his hand.

The sweet-spice tang of her own dragonness wafted now from her skin. Emory thought freedom was not so important. And he thought the dragon was gone.

How many other ways, Ama wondered, was Emory wrong?

"You tricked me back in my lair," Ama said.

"Not hard," Emory countered. "I used my brain, that's all. My first weapon. Dragons cannot see shade or shadow. Only shine and light."

And then Ama saw, in a flash, her first home—the great amber orb from whence she had come—the sun, her beloved, a riotous monster of explosive flames. The sun, her own heart made large. She came from the orange-red fuzz of its curve; she came from the roil and boil of its skin; she came from the explosive jets of liquid flame; she came from the quiet dance of whorls and swirls; she came from its glitter and its shine; she came from its movement and its silence. She came from the rivers of plasma, the sprays of flaming crimson, the ribbons of copper, the constantly changing, living, breathing, beating, churning, yearning orb.

She was of the sun and from the sun. She was not a plaything of this little man.

"You stabbed me with your steel," Ama said.

"I did. My second weapon. I found the unprotected flesh beneath your arm. I pierced you good, I did."

Ama remembered the blade going in, the surprise of it. She saw herself biting at the wound, desperate to extract the metal from within her flesh. She felt her teeth connect with the sword's shaft, she remembered how it felt to pull it out, the rush and gush of blood that came with it.

"And then," said Ama.

"Yes," Emory said. "It takes three weapons to conquer a dragon and free a damsel. My brain. My steel. And my yard."

Ama's End

"Your yard," Ama said.

"You should thank me," Emory repeated. "You—the dragon—managed to extract the steel. The dragon lay and bled, but I knew it would not be long before it rose again, and my sword was gone, so the next time it attacked, I would be done for. There was nothing to lose by trying. And Mother had told me that it takes three weapons to slay a dragon. My yard, I have with me, always.

"Of course," Emory continued, "a dragon is not female in the same ways as a woman. They are singular creatures. They do not eat, but get their strength from sunlight. They do not mate or birth. One a generation, that is all. One dragon, one damsel. You were my destiny, Ama. I had to take you. I went to the dragon's lair to find a damsel. I would leave with one."

"You . . . improvised," Ama said, remembering. She had lain

bleeding on the stone floor of her lair, rose-tinted mirrors all around, her gems and jewels scattered into disaster. And here came Emory, loosening the buckle of his belt, freeing the horn of him, and entering the bloody tear he had ripped beneath her arm.

Then there was nothing. No more, no memory, until she opened new eyes to find herself in his arms, in his saddle, in his possession.

"I made you beautiful," Emory said again, again.

"You keep saying that," Ama answered. "But I did not ask for your beauty. I made beauty all on my own. I did not need you then."

"You need me now," Emory said. "I am your destiny, as much as you are mine. Now, enough of this. It matters not where you came from, or what I did to bring you here. All that matters is what we shall do. And that is this: We shall forget all this nonsense. The glassblower shall sweep up this mess of broken glass, and I shall deliver you to your girl, who will dress you for the wedding. And we shall meet at the altar, and be wed, and I shall be king, and you, queen, and you shall birth me a son, and you shall find all the beauty you have need of in my arms and in his eyes. For that is the way it has always been, and that is the way it shall always be, from the beginning of time to the end of it."

The scent of Ama's own sweet-spice tang, the rush of her blood, hot now, near to boiling, the knowledge of the truth of her—these things she would need to set aside to do as Emory commanded.

It was true, what Emory said: as long as there had been kings, there had been conquered dragons and damsels brought from their lair.

Not rescued, though. Stolen.

"I think," Ama said, "that I do not wish to marry you. Or to be queen. I want none of it."

"Girl," Emory said, "it matters little what you *want*. Remember your Sorrow—or your Fury, if you'd rather—for if you give me trouble on this count, or any other, she shall be hunted until dead. I promise you that."

"Grant me leave and promise not to hunt my Fury," Ama said. "Do these things, and I shall go in peace."

"You seem to be under some misguided impression that you have power here," Emory said slowly, as if he spoke to a young child. "But you are wrong."

Slowly, Ama knelt. And when she rose again, she clutched in her hand a sickle-sharp spire of glass. "I, too, have three weapons," she said. "And glass is but one of them."

"Enough," Emory spat, and he lunged at her, fist connecting with her temple. Pain shot through Ama's head, her vision went to stars, but she held her space and did not fall. Her hand clenched the glass, blood poured from her palm, but she did not waver.

"Strike me again," Ama said. An invitation? A threat?

It mattered not. Emory lunged again, and this time, she was quicker, deftly sidestepping his fist, the spike-sharp tip of her weapon entering his chest just beneath his rib cage. She drew it upward like a filleting knife, opening Emory wide.

He stumbled back, his mouth in a surprised round O, hands reaching up to try to close himself like a jacket, but his life's blood spilling, pouring, and he fell to the ground among the splintered remains of Ama's self-portrait.

"One should not make a pet out of a wild beast," Ama said. She mounted Emory, knelt over him, and, ignoring his batting, bloodied hands, she reached into his chest, pulled open his mortal wound, and extracted his still-beating heart.

It pulsed in her palm, and Ama bit into it like a ripe plum.

In the chapel, all the king's men were gathered and waiting for the ceremony to begin.

In the kitchen, the cooks and scullery maids worked to arrange a fine feast for their king.

In the great hall, the musicians sat, instruments in hand.

In Ama's room, Tillie waited for the return of her mistress.

And in her bed, surrounded by cats, the queen mother watched through her window as a great opaline dragon cut across the sky and disappeared, singular, into the night.

Acknowledgments

This book began on a rooftop in San Francisco, with a gift of words from a brilliant friend. I want to thank MaryLynn Reise for the generous loan of the rooftop (and the apartment beneath) and Martha Brockenbrough for the inspiration.

As a mother to two human children and seven nonhumans, my leaving town, even for the rooftops of San Francisco, is not possible without the assistance of Karen and Ted Negus, whose support enables me to sneak out of town to write. Thank you.

I'm endlessly grateful for the love and support of my siblings, my husband, and my children.

I'll never tire of acknowledging my agent and friend, Rubin Pfeffer, who has been my steadfast partner since 2011, or my wonderful editor, Jordan Brown, whose enthusiasm and care for my writing buoys me every day; working with both of you is a pleasure and a privilege.

And finally, the team at Balzer + Bray has astounded me. I'm so grateful to Alessandra Balzer, Donna Bray, Tiara Kittrell, Michelle Taormina, Alison Donalty, Bethany Reis, Bess Braswell, Sabrina Abballe, Meg Beatie, Allison Brown, Kate Jackson, Suzanne Murphy, and the artists of Vault49 for helping *Damsel* manifest. Dragons are singular creatures, but authors are not, and I am deeply thankful for you all.